FIERY
BLESSING

Hermosa Beach Memoirs #2

Danube Adele

DANUBE ADELE

COPYRIGHT

This is a work of fiction. Any
resemblance to actual persons, living
or dead, business establishments,
events or locales is entirely
coincidental. All rights reserved.
Except for use in a review, the
reproduction or use of this work in any
part is forbidden without the express
written permission of the author.

Dedication

To my sweetheart—once we met,
the magic began.

ACKNOWLEDGEMENTS

I want to give a big shout out to my best friend, Kiese Hill, who has been a great source of encouragement. In spite of her own load of work, she is always happy to read chapters I send her. She also gives me real, authentic feedback to help me write the best story I can. Through the good times and the painful ones, she has been a rock, and I can't thank her enough.

Another big 'thank you' belongs to Thalia Sutton, my copy editor, for fitting me into her schedule with very short notice. My family received sudden, devastating, medical news that has us dealing with challenges for a long time. This book was put to the side until I was nearly out of time, so I do appreciate Thalia's willingness to jump on this work for me.

Chapter 1
Ian

"Get. The. Fuck. Off. Of. Me!"

Sharp. Angry. Female.

The words were loud and clear, as if shouted from right next to me. But where was the voice coming from?

I was scowling into my fridge with the overly bright inner light piercing my eyeballs, wondering what the hell was going on. Early morning brain fog had me blurry-eyed and confused. I shot a glance around the kitchen.

"You think you're so damn cute, but you're not!" Definitely an irate woman. Was that my new sexpot neighbor? It had to be. Damn. It sounded like a lovers' spat. Strange. I hadn't seen a guy hanging out, but that didn't mean there wasn't one.

The thought was involuntarily souring, not that I

was seriously interested in her; that was not a part of the plan. That wasn't why I was here. I'd learned the golden rule: Never do your fun where you do your work. Not that she knew she was work. Not yet.

But she was sexy as fuck.

It didn't hurt to look. Appreciate. Enjoy.

Watching her prance her cute little cosplay ass around on her balcony over the last couple of weeks had been pure pleasure. Yesterday, she'd been a female version of Indiana Jones, everything feminine and fitted, showing off all of my favorite parts on a woman. The day before, she'd been a psychedelic go-go dancer with a short skirt that showed plenty of long leg on top of platform boots.

"Leave me alone!"

I winced against her shout.

Nice pair of lungs. Nice pair of tits, too.

She'd caught me checking her out a few times. The first was a week ago. Standing just inside my sliding glass door, I'd been about to come out on the large, roof patio that we shared. Seeing me there, she'd struck a poster-girl pose beside her teak chair—back arched so her full, perky, breasts were pushed out, hand cocked on her hip. That made my dick jerk with surprise.

Yeah. I kept staring at that point.

She'd blown me a kiss through full lips and completed a pageant girl wave goodbye before disappearing inside her own set of glass doors on her side of the patio. I thought there was even a whip hanging off her hip. For fuck's sake. The images that brought on...

Still, the memory of her audacity spread a sleepy smirk across my face. The moment begged the question, what kind of panties did a female archeologist wear, if any? Unfortunately, it seemed I wouldn't be finding out anytime soon. There was genuine regret in knowing that.

I was here to work a deal. Negotiate. Get the contract signed. Bring her onboard. It was what I was good at. Maybe then, this personal Glitch I'd been experiencing, the sudden apathy I was plagued with, would disappear. Things could go back to normal again.

The new CEO position of Gamecon was mine. Everyone knew it, and if my instincts were right, which they always were, this new acquisition would cement it. This was going to be the deal of a century, the next global phenomena. It could have the same success of Minecraft or GTA which netted billions worldwide. I could see it.

Climbing to the top to lead this company was the plan. It had been the plan since I first started working for the company seven years ago.

My contributions over the last several years had allowed the company to enter the upper echelons, becoming one of the top five gaming companies once again. My vision had steered us all toward exponential levels of success. This was essentially my company, and this new deal was set to be epic.

The problem?

The new job title held no excitement for me. Apathy.

I'd realized this little epiphany as I was visiting my kitchen this morning, thinking about what was coming down the pike, and I realized I could give a shit. This ultimately begged the question: What the hell was wrong with me?

This was part of what I was officially calling "The Glitch."

A rogue voice bubbled up from a deep, dark well in what I could only imagine was my subconscious, asked when I'd do something that I wanted to be doing, something that made me happy.

That also had to be part of the temporary personal glitch. Maybe I needed more rest.

Besides, happiness was temporary. An emotion for toddlers and trust fund douches. What was more important was the power I'd built, the connections I'd solidified, the financial independence I'd amassed.

Fuck happy.

Better to stick with the plan.

The plan was to make initial contact tomorrow. Invite a formal meeting in my new office space downstairs. Discuss the details, the future outlook.

What Gamecon could do for her with the capital we could infuse into the process of testing, publication, and distribution. There was no way she could say no.

"Dammit!"

So why did her voice sound like she was in the same room? Her words had come across clearly.

"No!"

The orange juice was sitting on the shelf, one of the few items I'd grabbed at the corner mom-and-pop market the previous night. The cold air from the fridge reminded me that I had disgusting cottonmouth and a dull ache behind my eyes. I grabbed the carton, needing to soothe the dryness in my throat.

The gaming industry was a global business. Clients all over the world. The sun never set in this industry. It was the motto that had led me to the power seat I found myself in at the company. That and never trust anyone. Not a single, goddamn person. Except my mom.

"Let go of my pants! Let go!"

Swigging from the carton and swiping my chin, almost in the same move, I replaced it, closed the fridge, and cocked my head toward the sound of her voice. Scratching at my chest absently, I wondered if there was a vent between our apartments. Being that I had the south side of the building while she had the north, I knew we shared a long wall, but being an old building, I figured it had thicker walls.

Could she hear me as clearly? Because that would be…

"Let go of my pants, you bastard! Get off of me! Now!"

And that's when I realized she was being attacked.

Adrenaline shot through my system. Shoving past the furniture, I launched out of my apartment.

God save any motherfucker that forced her to do anything because he was going to get hulk slammed.

Deaf to everything but blood roaring through my ears, I flew across the short foyer between our apartments and kicked open her front door. Wood splintered from around the door frame, pieces of it exploding inward. Shoving the door out of my way as it bounced back off the opposite wall, I stepped into the room and looked for danger, my breath coming in panting huffs, muscles tensed.

"What…" she yipped, head snapping my direction.

There was no danger.

Everything was summed up in a fraction of a second. There was a very large, black-and-tan dog playing tug-o-war with a pair of pants. The owner of the pants, my little, blonde, bombshell neighbor, was, unfortunately, partially wearing those pants. They were halfway up her thighs, and she was bouncing on one leg while the dog yanked on an empty cuff.

She stared at me with her big blue eyes, so light they were almost gray, rounded in surprise. This moment of distraction, however, gave the large pooch enough of an advantage that he won the tug-o-war instantly. With a victorious yank, the dog knocked her off her feet and then stood there triumphantly, her pants in his mouth.

Meanwhile, my sexpot neighbor sat sprawled, legs splayed open. It gave me a great view of her girly panties, which answered my burning question from earlier: No, female Indiana Jones did not go commando. She wore sexy panties. Barely-there panties.

And the dog stood proudly.

Yes. She was now pant less.

I couldn't say I hated this.

She jumped up to her feet, squinting and glaring in equal measure at me and the dog, shapely legs under a set of nice, rounded tits that were heaving in her tank top. Her long blonde hair, nearly platinum in color, was tied back in a sleek ponytail.

"What the hell were you thinking?" she blasted.

"Are you talking to me or the dog?" I asked, because seriously, I wasn't sure where she was directing her anger.

"Both of you!" she snarled, hands on her hips. No shame. No embarrassment. I respected that. She spun on the dog. "Some scary dog you are. Aren't you supposed to be a Rottweiler or something? Give me my fucking pants you worthless beast!"

"Me, or the dog?"

"The dog!" She threw her hands up with frustration.

"You know he can't understand, right?"

She rolled her eyes and moved toward the dog, who danced away grinning his doggy grin, begging for her to chase him.

"Dammit!" she charged after him, giving him exactly what he wanted, and giving me a sight to behold. A gorgeous, heart shaped ass, encased in some flowery thong, flashed me as she dove after the squirrely animal, trying to trap him around the furniture. He kept escaping her.

If I were being very, very smart, I would remember why this was a bad way to present myself to a new client and get my ass out of this gorgeous woman's apartment as soon as I could. Let her figure out the whole dog situation because it was hardly a way to start a professional relationship. We'd never officially met, but it was like we were having an underwear party, which was not how I pictured us meeting for the first time.

If I was being completely honest, my feet were planted. Stuck fast. Frozen in place, watching her chase the dog. She'd fascinated me from the first moment I'd known of her, seen her in pictures, and here she was in the same room. Almost naked.

I silently cheered him on.

Was my lack of professionalism more evidence of the glitch?

But this was better stimulation than coffee any day of the week.

"Where are your glasses? Can you see him?" I asked casually, realizing why she was squinting so hard. I'd usually seen her wearing a pair. It was adorable, not that I was about to say this out loud. She'd probably kick me in the balls for admitting that to her.

"Help me out here, don't just stand there." She tossed me her cute "angry" look. A definite "mad kitten" face. Was that a thing? If not, it was now.

I suddenly pushed further into the room to grab the fleeing animal precisely as she jumped to corner it from the opposite direction.

We ran straight into each other.

Full body. Skin-to-skin.

That moment was the catalyst.

The start of the chemical reaction.

Instant sparks.

Funny how things can happen in a fraction of a second.

My arms came around her, holding her steady. Small, soft hands were braced on my pecs, squeezing, giving me instant goosebumps up my neck. Heat suddenly infused my veins and arrowed south to the monster. Then I realized where I was grabbing.

One of my hands had landed on her lower back, but the other had landed on her ass cheek, cupped it reflexively. Massaged supple flesh before I thought better of it. She fit perfectly; her small, lush form pressed into me.

Her eyes were wide, blinking up at me for a few seconds of surprise, the moment seemingly frozen in time, before a wicked gleam entered their pale blue depths. Like she was thinking about things. Dirty things. I saw it happen in real time.

Instantly, my dick was growing hot and heavy. And she could feel it.

Realizing this, I swiftly jerked away. My face warmed. Was that a blush? Was I blushing? I needed to correct this goddamn glitch. This was not me.

Her soft blues danced upward, her lips quirked off-center in her own smirk before she said, "Aren't you a delicious ride from Fantasyland."

How was I supposed to respond to that?

This was not how I'd wanted to introduce myself. Luckily, she saved me from having to respond. By the way, I had no response—and when had I ever been speechless? In my life, I was gifted with the right thing to say. Always. Except now. Glitch. It was the only explanation.

"Help me, would you?" Her scowl was back on

the dog. She'd pulled away to square up with him again. "I need my pants, dog."

Noting she was creeping up on the dog from one direction, I went the other, and he was finally cornered, trapped between a coffee table and the couch. He crouched down, gave a growling, muffled bark, and I knew he was moments away from jumping over or even onto the coffee table.

Using my deepest, most ferocious, no-nonsense CEO tone, I growled, "Drop it. Now!"

The dog looked up at me, surprised.

Paused for a moment to stare into my eyes. Blinked a few times. Relaxed his jaws infinitesimally.

And dropped the pants.

He managed to look guilty and remorseful at the same time.

"Good boy," I murmured. He turned dark, loving eyes up at me, let his tongue loll out the side of his mouth.

Sweet sexpot girl stared down at the dog for a moment, dumbfounded. Then she threw a scowl my direction before turning it back on the dog.

"Really?" Exasperation underscored every jerking motion of her arm as she snagged up her pants, turned away from me, and yanked them up her legs, hiding the sweet curve of her ass that I realized I was staring at, before zipping up and turning back around. She squinted down at the pooch. "You're a bad dog."

"He looks like a puppy," I offered, wondering if I needed to apologize for staring at her ass, having my hand on her ass. Her soft, round ass. The monster jerked again, and I wanted to shake my head. Where was my self-control? They called me Shark around the office. Whispered it behind my back, but I knew. Nothing happened that I didn't know about. Shark. Cold. Emotionless. I was proud of that.

So why did I feel like the situation was totally out of my control?

I was off my game.

I needed to get the hell out of here. Refocus. Rework my plan for starting this partnership off on the right foot.

"How can he be a puppy. He's like, over a hundred pounds," she grumped, clearly exasperated. She scanned the room, scowling, her hands jammed on her hips.

"You don't know for sure?" I asked, wondering what she was doing now.

Her eyes continued to search the area a beat longer before she huffed yet another aggravated breath, finally throwing her arms up. "Where the hell are my glasses? I'm fucking blind. I can't see to find them. They got dislodged when I was fighting off the Kraken, here."

"Hold on." In a microsecond scan of the room, I

saw they were flung open on the arm of an overstuffed chair opposite the couch and worked my way around the huge pooch who was determined to keep stepping in front of me, hoping for more pets.

Peripherally, I saw it was a nice, casually elegant space. Wooden floors. Comfy-looking overstuffed couch set with chocolate-colored upholstery facing a large entertainment unit with a huge television that covered one wall. Gaming paraphernalia was strewn about, and I wondered what she played in her free time. It said a lot about someone, in my business.

Grabbing her glasses, I handed them over. Caught a whiff of oranges. Drew her scent into my lungs.

Of course she smelled good. Delicious. And she felt good. And she looked good.

"Thanks," she sighed.

She started cleaning them with the bottom of her shirt, flashing smooth, pale skin around her belly button. It also looked soft. Touchable. I realized she was still talking and tuned back in with a mental shake of my head.

Shark, Ian. Think Shark.

"…anyway, my nephews brought him in when they showed up last night, and now they're in class, and I don't want to text them because it might get them in trouble with their teachers. I was too busy to ask questions. I now realize I should have. They didn't bring his food, a leash, or anything." She finally put her glasses on and took a deep breath, studying the dog. "I'm about to go buy him some food. So, you think he's a puppy? Should I get puppy chow or something?"

"Talk with the guys at the pet store. There's all kinds of food for different ages and sizes of dog." The beast was calming down. He had a short stub of a tail that was wagging madly as his eyes flicked between the two of us, waiting for a clue to our next game.

In an ideal world, he wouldn't be part of our next game. Neither would her pants.

But I could not fuck her. Shark, Ian. Shark. Focus.

"And you are in your boxers?" She was now looking down at my dick that was still at half-mast. Partly, I was gratified to see her eyes widen with what looked like appreciation at the same time I felt that dull flush hit my neck again. Fuck me. Another blush.

Since when did I blush? Fucking glitch.

"I thought someone was attacking you. I heard you yelling next door."

"Well," she arched her brows consideringly, her eyes lingering on my cock a beat longer before looking up at me. "I guess I should thank you? If someone were attacking me, you would have saved me, Mr. Eye Candy."

"Eye Candy?" That startled a grin from me. Considering I'd been checking out her tits and ass, I couldn't protest. "I like that. Especially since I've been secretly calling you Sexpot."

"Sexpot?" she laughed, and her face lit up. "I like it. Sexpot it is. And while we seem to be the most informal of strangers, you know, running around in our underwear together during our first meeting, it might be good to know what else you are called. In case the delivery man shows up with a package for you."

"Right. They won't be looking for Mr. Eye Candy."

"Nor Ms. Sexpot, either."

"Ian."

She shook my outstretched hand. It was small and soft. Engulfed by my grasp. Knowing how soft her other parts were didn't help the situation in my boxers. My dick liked the idea of exploring all of her soft places. She'd been the source of endless fascination for me, and I was finally talking to her.

It was time for me to head back before my cock pointed due north, even though I was gratified to see that I was not the only one affected.

Her own cheeks pinkened, and she pulled her hand away quickly, saying, "Ian. You're the guy making all the noise next door when I'm trying to work."

It didn't escape my notice that she was crossing her arms to shield her breasts from my gaze, but it was too late. Of course, I noticed her nipples had gone hard in her flimsy tank. I'm a guy. I pay attention to these things, even if I would not act on them. And I wouldn't. Even if grabbing her ass had given me a proprietary feeling.

"Guilty," I shrugged. "Sorry for that."

"Yeah, well, I'm trying to meet a deadline, and you're fucking up my schedule with your noisage, Mr. Eye Candy." She forced a scowl.

"What are you working on?"

"Just, some tech projects." She looked down at the dog with a sigh. "I still need to buy him some stuff. He probably needs a walk or something, right? Shit. I don't have time for this. I don't know why my sister didn't mention the dog before doing a drop-and-run. But hey, are you about done over there?"

"About. A few odds and ends left. I can arrange the time to better suit you."

"That would be great. I work late and get up late. Except for this week. My nephews are staying with me." She sighed a groan. "How can boys be so messy in less than a twelve-hour period?"

"Talent?"

"Maybe." She shuffled toward the splintered door, and I followed behind. Yes, my eyes were glued to her ass again. It was going to be harder not to look now that I knew what she was hiding under the denim. Knew how it fit in my palm. Again, I realized she was still talking and tuned back in. "...I amend that. Boys can be messy in minutes of showing up. Is that my door, shredded off the hinge?"

"It is. I'll send someone over to fix it today if that's all right."

"I'd appreciate that. By the way, my name's Blessing."

"Nice to meet you."

"Now we won't be strangers."

"No, we won't."

But I already knew her name.

In fact, she was the reason I'd moved in to begin with.

Chapter 2
Blessing

The spark was real.

I'd felt it. Sizzling. Smoking. Turn-the-oven-off because I was done kind of hot. This was not my imagination. And it was…a surprise. Instant explosion of chemistry? Immediate urge to climb a guy like he was a jungle gym? Never had it happened before.

He kicked in my goddamn door like a boss, like a…dare I say it? Superhero. Be still my heart. Took up the whole doorway with his size. *Like the Hulk*, my girly hearts-and-flowers voice whispered inwardly on a sigh. My favorite superhero. Of course, without the whole being green thing, not that I would have held that against him.

There were other things I wanted held up against me, though. Big things. Sexy things. A treasure trail that needed to be explored. Those amazing muscles that angled in a "V", as though, perhaps, pointing an avid, eager explorer south. I sighed.

Large man, muscles heaving like a dark avenging angel. Holy fucking cow, he was hot. Hotter than hot. Panty-wetting kind of hot. A slow smolder ending in a much-needed screw kind of hot. Whew!

I was still getting over the sight.

And his voice? When he used his big-man alpha voice to get Kraken to obey, I bit back a groan. But when we touched? Let's just say it would not have taken much more for me to come spontaneously.

Change of panties needed?

Most definitely.

Maybe that would be his new nickname.

And now I knew I his eye color: Aquamarine. Not quite blue, not quite green. Sharp. Vibrant. Piercing in their focus and singularity of purpose. They were startling, surrounded by the blue-black quality of his mussed hair, beard scruff, brows, and lashes.

And he was definitely packing. His big hand on my ass had held on tight for a split second. The outline of his package pressed against my belly was impressive enough to make me want to whimper.

Mr. Eye Candy. Or was Mr. Panty-wetter a better moniker? No. Just Hulk. That really said it all, didn't it? Something to think about.

"You have to buy what?" Layla asked, pulling me from my lovely, triple-X mental distraction. She cut a glance over her shoulder from her workspace as I grabbed coffee "to go" from the small kitchenette area I'd installed in the office.

Our web design business was housed on the second floor below my living space. I owned the north side of the top two floors of the building in downtown Hermosa Beach, only a few blocks inland. It had amazing views from the top floor.

Yes, I'm that girl. Born with some privilege. Not bottomless, confetti-like Paris Hilton money. Not fuck-it-all kind of money. Just some good extra. My parents would kick my ass if I ever sat around and waited to be taken care of. They'd taught me the value of hard work and earning my way in the world, but they'd also provided a leg up. A small trust fund that came to me at twenty-one.

Something they'd saved for me, just in case.

Because I was an "oops" baby.

Because they were older and had trouble keeping it in their pants when they thought no one could get pregnant anymore. I proved them wrong, wrong, wrong.

"Dog food. I have to run off and buy dog food," I muttered, thinking back to the situation I faced upstairs. I had shit to do. I didn't have time to drive all over town figuring out what a large, playful beast with big teeth needed. What the hell? A dog?

And it couldn't even be a cute little toy something or other. No. It was a freaking giant-ass beast.

The frustration made me sound cranky and out of sorts, which I hated. Sheesh. Do a good thing for someone and look what happens.

My sister and her husband snuck off for some nookie in Hawaii for their anniversary; meanwhile, I had a wild animal ravaging my living space without even a word of warning. Not a one.

"Dog food. Yeah, that's what I thought you said." Layla cocked her head, dark ponytail swinging behind her. She pivoted her office chair toward me to fully engage in this moment. Her dark blue eyes looked bemused. "Please tell me you're not on a special diet, or... wait. You aren't feeding your nephews dog food, are you? I mean, I know you don't have a lot of kid experience, but really. They eat people food." Her voice was grave, but she was also biting her lip to keep from smirking.

Layla had become quite the snarky one since getting her groove on with the hot military-vet-gym-club-owner, Mason. He, too, was a hottie who, clearly, (based on her boost of confidence) had magic in his pants, so it actually made sense.

I deadpanned back to her, not feeling quite that jovial. "No, smart-ass. I haven't started a dog food diet, and I know what to feed my nephews. The problem is my nephews brought a dog without bringing anything to take care of him. I have him blocked, sort of, upstairs. I don't think he can make his way down here…yet. I practically gave myself a hernia doing it, but I moved the smaller sectional in the way of the stairs. But now I've gotta go. I'm afraid he's going to eat my furniture if he gets hungry enough."

"A doggie?" she said, her voice rising like several octaves with a goofy I-love-creatures look coming over her face. "Awww."

"No, not a sweet little dog you can fawn over. A big-ass dog. A Kraken. In fact, that's what I'm going to start calling him since my nephews never told me his name." Thinking of my morning adventure, I took a breath. "And, in further news, I met our new neighbor."

"Mr. Hot Stuff?"

"Yeah. Flashed him my ass, my tits."

"That going to be your new normal greeting?" She raised her brows. "Just asking."

I explained instead of answering. "He'll be sending guys over to the top floor to repair the door he kicked off the hinges."

"What?" The grin she'd been fighting dropped instantly. There was some pleasure in that response, so I continued the mystery.

"He thought the Kraken was an attacker when, really, he was just trying to steal my pants off me, hence the flash of butt cheeks."

"What?! Kraken or Mr. Hot Stuff?" Even better.

The more I spoke, the more confused she became.

"And, I'm off. If you hear barking that is deep, growly, snarly, and frightening, you can ignore it. It's my beast upstairs. The four-legged one, at least."

"You have others?"

"Well, my nephews will be home after school. They count, right?"

And that was how I left her, and now I was wearing my own smile. It lasted only long enough to get in the car where I then had to battle morning rush hour/beach traffic while heading to the dog food store. Ugh. Animals were not my thing. They were messy. Unpredictable. Slobbery. At least Kraken was.

I cringed.

While I was lacing up my boots, he'd licked my cheek. A trail of dog spit had been left on my face without any shame. He just stared up at me with his big brown eyes, like I was the coolest thing since thick-cut fried bacon, or something.

But no. I mean, he was cute, but no. I did not like unruly, drooly creatures around me or my electronics. Right? Bad idea. Particularly ones that outweighed me.

"Talk to me, Spiderman." With traffic backing up on the narrow streets, I called my old friend and current game design partner, Pedro Ramirez, who happened to now be living in the Netherlands.

"How goes it?"

"Batman!" his voice crackled over the car speakers. "This is early for you. I didn't expect to hear from you until tonight, or what you would call lunch."

"Short version, I've got my sister's kids for a week. I had to get them up and give them breakfast at the butt-crack dawn of six thirty before shoving them out the door for school."

I huffed out a breath remembering the pain of opening my eyes to full awareness with a dog panting his hot breath in my face, and how my actual brain synapsis hurt from lack of proper rest. When was the last time I'd woken up already envisioning a nap for myself?

"You know how to cook?" came his snarky reply.

"I know how to pour." And microwave. Like a champ.

"Cereal, then. Let me guess. Peanut butter Captain Crunch?"

"I'm not their favorite aunt for nothing." Of course, I was their only aunt.

I appreciated his laughter since the morning traffic sucked. I'd otherwise be throwing unfriendly finger signs out the window and making snarly faces at everyone who wanted to drive like my grandma. No offense to my grandma. She actually kicked ass when she was still alive.

His exhausted exhale was deeply heartfelt across the ocean. "Yeah, I hear you."

"Let's talk again in a couple of days."

"All right. Maybe I'll have some good news for you by then. So…" He paused like he had a thought. "Hey, before you go, there's a game you should check out. It's a little dark. A little edgy. A little dated since it was first created like ten years ago, but it's cool and free on Steam. It's called *Terminus Wars: Survival*. It's a post-apocalyptic rebuilding society concept, a little rough, but worth it."

"I'll check it out. Steam. *Terminus Wars: Survival*." I finally turned into the strip mall, relieved that I'd been right about where I'd seen the damn pet store and parked in the lot. Attached to my console was my very convenient idea notepad, so I pulled into a spot near the door to the pet store, grabbed the pencil hanging from the pad and jotted it down. I always took up his suggestions. Pedro, Spiderman, had never steered me wrong. "Sounds good. Okay, then. I'm at the pet store. I've got to go."

"The pet store? You changing your diet or something?" he snorted. He knew my aversion to animals.

"You and Layla are so god damn funny, I forgot to laugh." At least this time I could smirk. "Good-bye."

"Later, B-girl."

If I thought the day was going to get better, maybe normalize a bit more, settle, allow me some time for some work, some socializing, and some general time wastage, I was totally wrong. I ended up back in the front seat of my little Fiat more than an hour later feeling like I'd been totally worked by the dude in the store as I sat amid a whirlwind of dog food, flea medication, chew toys, leashes, collars, and treats wondering what the hell cost so much money? This was dog stuff, not gold nuggets.

How could a dog bone cost more than a damn steak?

Traffic was worse, not better, and I had to stop myself from hulk-shouting rude epithets to the innocent people driving around me. Yes, I recognized they were just trying to get to their day jobs, but I couldn't help that I was not a morning person. Never had been.

Which was why I had no business driving before about noon, but today had not been a normal day. I mean, first there was Mr. Eye Candy himself, Hulk, with his sexy boxers. It wasn't usually the first question you could answer about a stranger. Of course, it wasn't usual for a stranger to kick your door in, either.

That was weird. Not the weirdest thing I'd seen, I mean, come on. Look at who I was here? Favorite superhero? I loved, loved the Hulk. I also loved dressing as all my favorite characters and tropes, gaming, and even making a damn video game. I'm one of the biggest tech nerds I know, and that's saying something since I lived in that world of role play, so no. Not the weirdest thing.

But, his door-kicking aside, Ian was most definitely easy on the eyes. Remembering our exchange from the morning kept my brain happily occupied long enough to get home without doing damage to an innocent bystander.

Especially not when the innocent bystander was that sexy guy with the hot, sweaty body, t-shirt and jogging shorts who'd just disappeared back inside our building.

My neighbor, the Hulk.

Chapter 3
Ian

I was fully tuned in to the sounds coming from Ms. Sexpot's apartment, so I knew the moment she returned.

"Hi honey! I'm home!" Blessing's voice, deliberately mocking television sitcoms, bled through the wall to someone else who was inside her apartment.

A few friendly barks echoed. A whine. A muttered rebuke. I smiled, thinking of the large K-9 currently housed with my bombshell neighbor.

Actually, bombshell seemed too tame a word. She was so much more. More than I'd imagined before coming here. More mesmerizing. More unpredictable. More impactful. Just…more. I hadn't expected that.

Not just a bombshell. Bomb blast. It better suited

who she was.

Or…just Blast. She seemed to be the reason I was blowing my well-ordered life up.

Maybe. I needed to think on it.

Or maybe I didn't.

Maybe it wasn't a good idea to think on it at all. What the hell was I doing risking the endgame? I'd run a goddamn marathon for so long, making painful sacrifices along the way, only to fuck it all up when I was on the final lap?

No way.

It was time to slide into home-plate, sprint the last lap, not smell the pretty roses. Even if those roses had long legs and gorgeous eyes that seemed to be laughing at my attempt to maintain the rules I'd established for myself.

Ridiculous. That was what this whole infatuation was. Absolutely ridiculous. Spontaneously buying the place next door to hers. What the hell was I thinking? We were not going to fuck around.

Wasn't going to happen.

I wouldn't let it.

Unfortunately, the memory of her snarky, lip-quirk-grin, how perfectly her ripe little body fit mine like a damn missing puzzle piece, and the outrageous way we met, floated through my mind still. Multiple times in the last hour, I'd thought about my hand on her ass, the sexy grin she'd thrown up at me, and the arousal I could read in her eyes. I'd spent the entire morning half erect, fully distracted, and with zero focus.

Why zero?

Because I kept listening for sounds of her through the wall instead of paying attention to the president of my company, Harvey Stephens, who was on a call with me. I had him on speaker.

The upside? My encounter with Blessing was distracting enough to keep me from telling him, finally, to go fuck himself, something I'd wanted to do from the first time I'd met him. I'd wanted to say *Fuck you, you fucking asshole, you'd be a lonely shit pile on the ground if not for your family trying to save your ass by handing you a company.*

I'd never been closer to it than now. Tip-of-my-tongue close. Making me nervous about my own knee-jerk reaction, close.

Part of the stupid glitch. Had to be.

I sighed. Kept listening.

"Josh has already pitched his next acquisition, and it's perfect. Real good. I'm about to make my final decision unless you give me something. And I mean now," Harvey demanded.

That caught my attention. The silence stretched a beat as I considered what he'd said.

"Are you threatening me, Harvey?" My voice barely notched above a low growl with the implications of his words.

"It's not a threat, Ian. It's a promise," Harvey

barked through the phone. "This is a business, and I don't have time for your bullshit sense of moral ethics. What the fuck is going on. Start talking!"

My jaw tightened before I deliberately took a moment to mindfully relax each muscle. Breathe. Watch the waves roll in from my third story window. Observe the surfers, more like dots on the horizon at this distance. They were bobbing peacefully on the moody blue waves, facing the gray misty morning while waiting for the right set to perk them up.

Maybe I could learn to surf. Find that peace that others seemed to discover so easily but which had always seemed a luxury to me. The idea held strong appeal.

Meanwhile, I had to play this game, live out this reality. Listen to this blowhard who knew nothing about our industry except that his uncle had done the equivalent of giving him the keys to a high-performance sports car when he didn't know how to drive a stick. Yeah, give your middle-aged failure of a nephew the company.

As the current president he also decided the next CEO since our last one, Rick Montoya, had resigned citing health issues. The board would go along with whomever Harvey chose.

But here was the strange part: I didn't seem to have any anxiety over it, which was the issue that was most noteworthy. Again, total apathy.

I'd had my eye on this job since I'd graduated. It was within my reach, and I couldn't seem to give a shit anymore.

Glitch.

"Did you hear what I said?"

"I'm sure you're going to make the best choice, and we both know Josh can barely find his ass with both hands. He wouldn't know a good acquisition if it punched him in the nuts."

Harvey sputtered. Interesting to note that he was clearly Team Josh. "I don't know what you're talking about. Josh has been working his ass off."

"That's what he's told you, I'm sure." I felt like being provoking. It worked.

"Listen up! Unless you have something for me, he's going to be my pick…" Harvey snarled over the line. He liked feeling like a big man, throwing his weight around, thinking he had some kind of control over me. He didn't. Not even close. But he was too stupid to realize it.

"Maybe you need to listen, Harvey. If you're already going to give that tool the position, then I won't be bringing any new clients into the fold. End of story. There's no way in hell I'm going to subject them to Josh's ineptitude."

"Are you threatening me?" he sputtered. I smirked.

"I'm keeping you in the loop."

"Josh thinks you're just fucking around to buy

some time."

"Why would I give a shit what Josh thinks?"

"All I know is that he keeps me informed, and I expect you to do the same."

Part of my personal mission had been to find the company's initial roots. Their cutting-edge innovations that had driven them in the beginning. Bring that star quality back online, to once again lead the pack. It was an ambitious fight I'd taken on. What was it now, seven years I'd been with the company? I'd signed on at age twenty-four and had hit the ground sprinting.

I hadn't stopped yet.

I took a deep breath, inhaling the salty ocean breeze through the open window. Brought it into my lungs for a beat and exhaled quietly before responding.

"That's unfortunate, Harvey. I can't give you details now, but you're going to miss out on what I think is an absolutely epic opportunity," I said in an even voice, knowing that he was doing his best to piss me off. "Maybe I'll have to let this one slide. VisiStation is looking for the next best RPG. They are a growing company, as I've been very recently…assured."

It didn't hurt to let him know I had options. The bastard knew I was the man for the job, the guy making the wheels turn on this machine, which I'd shown over and over again. And if he didn't know, what the hell was he spending his time on all day? Did Josh have dirt on him?

Josh Henderson, my supposed competitor, was a hack when it came to knowing the industry. He was, however, an excellent bullshitter, telling Harvey what he wanted to hear.

Josh had limited skills—I knew this because he'd managed to get into my general files on my private server. Of course, those were the dummy files I'd set up, and he'd left his digital footprint everywhere, looking through all the fake documents.

I'd already updated those dummy files to download a nasty, brute-force virus for the next time he decided to invade my private files. There was one file labeled "New Projects" just waiting for him. Nothing too astronomical, but he wouldn't see it coming.

He was also a tool of the first order, more interested in the promise of power in this billion-dollar industry than in having an appreciation for the artistry, the creativity, the moral quests of game play, the quality of the characters' learning potential. It was probably why he and Harvey were tight. Harvey had no integrity; he just liked having his ass kissed.

So why would I bring Blessing's game into his company under those conditions?

I had to say, I missed playing in the creative

sandbox of design. Once upon a time, in what felt like a galaxy far, far away, I'd put together my own games...

That was why I was so intrigued by Blessing Mendoza's work. It had reawakened a part of me that I'd had to subvert. As stupid as it sounded, it was like I could see the world again, the same way I had before signing on with Gamecon—before I'd been submerged in the disappointment of recognizing a slice of the industry I'd never seen before. The bloodsucking parasitic side.

But I could forgive myself.

Back in those days, I'd needed the money. To keep spending time fucking around with shit like creative design that didn't guarantee a paycheck was a luxury I didn't have, so I'd concentrated on the business end of it all.

"I'm tired of this bullshit, Ian. I don't have time for goddamn cloak-and-dagger games. Fucking convince me already," Harvey insisted, trying to force my hand. "What the fuck am I supposed to be waiting for?"

"You'll have to trust me," I replied. "All I can tell you is that I've discovered the next world-wide game play. I'll tell you more when I can."

"What the fuck?"

"I've always come through."

"With conditions. You changed the last contract for World Battle which affected our profit margin.

Chris Bower had the right to veto toy creation when it was time to draw up contracts. It was a fucking shit show of epic proportions."

I'd changed all of my contracts. Harvey just hadn't bothered to look at them, and Rick Montoya had signed every last one of them, making them official. He'd been my mentor. Hired me before the ink was dry on my Master's degree. We'd been of like minds. I was sorry to see him go.

"Chris was protecting his artistry and his investment."

"My investment," Harvey half-growled, half-yelled, more of his frustration bleeding through. "The company's investment. You want to change things around, and suddenly, we're losing money left and right. Hemorrhaging from our god damn assholes!"

"I'm sure that's what Josh told you? Did he tell you the part where Chris was going to walk with his game and give it to VisiStation? He stayed with us because I offered him protection."

My brief bark of laughter had no humor. I wondered why I was bothering with an explanation. He was told what he wanted to hear by Josh; once that happened, Harvey wouldn't hear anything else.

But this was about me. Not Harvey. I was realizing that this had the looks of a crossroads. Would he make the smart decision for CEO, or would he take his chances with the known bullshitter because the bottom line was this: I wouldn't stay with the company if Josh was in charge of our daily operations.

I was already being headhunted by other companies looking to bring me on, including VisiStation.

And for that reason, this next part of the conversation was a litmus test. For Harvey.

"Josh wanted to dismantle some of the game functions that were a crucial signature of the game, and we told him to fuck off. Then, Chris and I got a contract signed with Snap Blocks to create building sets of scenes from the game. Kids will grow up with these characters. We'll be nurturing our future players from childhood."

"Josh said they weren't necessary aspects of the game!" Harvey insisted. "We could have that game up and running in a few days, but your contract is keeping us from getting started with production."

"And this is how you know he's full of shit. I have a meeting tomorrow to sign that contract. It'll make the game profitable for years to come."

"Maybe. It's all a pretty story. You're gambling on potential," he challenged, and it was like talking to a child. He was going to argue rather than listen.

"Yes, Harvey," I said in a voice I would reserve for a five-year-old. "That's what we do. Gamble on potential. Since when is a game a guaranteed success?"

"And he has an opt-out clause."

"Which means we have to be motivated to keep him. We also have a responsibility to maintain a good relationship with the designers. If you want to stay relevant, have access to the best up-and-coming games, you can't piss off the people that make them. If you can wait, I'll have something for you in a couple of days."

"Fine. I'll wait. But I won't wait forever," he huffed, his impatience sharp. "So, not even a hint of what you're working on?"

"I've got a meeting to take before I bring this to you, but it will be worth it." That was my next problem to solve—Blessing didn't know who I was. Telling her at this point was going to be awkward; it required a delicate touch. Finesse. I hadn't figured it out yet.

What I knew for sure was that her work had affected me in a way I hadn't been affected in a long time. The little bit I'd managed to see kept me coming back, wanting to help bring this to life. Birth it to the market. The world she'd created was mesmerizing. Just like her.

I wanted more.

"We'll see," I heard Harvey grunt. I'd briefly forgotten he was still on the line. He hung up without another word, but I was used to that.

The tension in my shoulders and neck eased by degrees. This was my life. More and more, I realized I'd been sucked into the black, heartless void, but it was time to change the shit I could. Whatever couldn't be changed? Well, we'd just have to see what that looked like when it all shook out in the end.

I turned back to the kitchen, snagging the bottle of water that was sweating on the granite counter, managing to down half of it in one shot. I'd taken a run on the beach after my interaction with Bomb Blast Blessing earlier. The weather was perfect. A little cloudy. Chilled air since it was mid-December. Perfect for outdoor exercise.

Rivulets of sweat were still soaking my shirt, so I set the bottle down and grasped the neck to pull it off. Used it to wipe off my face, neck, chest before tossing it toward the washer in the kitchen alcove.

Harvey had called within moments of my return, and as always, talking with him left a stink to the air, along with the same question I found myself asking more and more frequently:

What the fuck was I doing working for such a douche? Even as CEO, he would still be the president.

Fucking hated that guy. In the beginning, that hadn't mattered. What had mattered was that right out of grad school, I'd received the golden ticket. Landed the dream job at one of the oldest, most established gaming company as soon as my degree was earned. Started making the kind of money that would not only pay off the loans my scholarship hadn't covered but give my mother a fighting chance. She'd worked her ass off as a single mom to provide for me.

Now, I needed to take care of her. But did I still need to keep the same poverty-stricken mentality that had driven me in the first place, or could I finally ease off the gas pedal? With that thought, my heart kicked up, beat faster. A mild anxiety was suddenly making me tense. I tried shoving it off to the side. It happened every time I considered a major change in my life. What if she got sick again? The work was crucial.

"Talk to me," I growled when my phone rang. I was a popular guy this morning.

The fact that my personal assistant, Sal, was calling told me something was going on. He always waited for me to call him to do a rundown of our daily schedule, so it had to be something significant. He was still working out of our home office in the bay area.

"Got a minute?" he clipped, keeping his voice quiet, like he was trying to stop from being overheard.

"Yeah. What's up?" I recapped my water bottle.

"Josh is now supposed to be part of the final follow-up meeting we have with Chris and Snap Blocks tomorrow. Harvey Stephens called, literally, one minute ago and said to make it happen," Sal warned.

"Why now?" I wondered.

"It was on your calendar on the company network," Sal offered. "Just like the rest of your meetings."

"Of course, but he's never been interested before."

"Josh and Harvey want our notes on everything we've done so far with Snap Blocks. They want to know who the contact person is and copies of the contracts in place. I just got off the phone with him. Wanted to give you a heads up."

"Fucking bastards," I muttered.

"Totally. Honestly, man, Josh is a slimy motherfucker. He's trying something here. I wouldn't trust him with his own mother's life at this point." His disdain came across clearly. "He's come by a few times in the morning this week. Tries to shoot the shit with me while I'm working. Check out what I'm doing."

"What does he talk about?"

"What games I'm playing in my free time, like we're bros or some shit. He acts like he knows all the games, but a few times, just to fuck with him, I made shit up. Pulled game titles out of my ass to see what he'd do. He just goes with it."

A brief, dark chuckle escaped, but it wasn't a sound of amusement. "He's been trying some ineffective espionage shit for the last year. He's working to get CEO."

"Yeah, well, check this out. I forgot my jacket on my chair yesterday. It was raining and fucking cold as balls when I got down to street level, so I went back up to the office to get it, and he was sitting at my desk trying to fuck with my computer."

"Sounds about right."

"I was like, 'Hey man, what's up?' He tells me straight to my face that he just came by looking for me. Saw my computer was on and was going to turn it off or some shit. Total bullshit. I always shut it off every night before I leave. I don't know what's happening, but since you moved south to work remotely, Josh has been doing some shady shit, and he isn't alone."

"Sounds like it. I can't say I'm surprised. Unfortunately."

It was time to call Chris. Postpone this meeting for a week until I got the lay of the land. I had a good relationship with the representatives from Snap Blocks, so I wasn't worried they would back out on us. However, it did sound like Josh's bullshit was actually company sanctioned.

Harvey was going to promote him. I was now pretty sure of it.

This was the first time Josh had decided to horn in on a meeting. It was significant. The fact that Harvey was trying to force this issue was the most important part of this meeting.

What did he think Josh was going to do? What had Josh told him he could do?

A quick mental scan of the contracts told me that Chris was ultimately safe, especially since I kept copies, both digital and printed, of the original paperwork that was signed. I needed to make sure he didn't sign anything else.

I made an executive decision.

"All right. I'm cancelling the meeting for tomorrow. Wait about an hour before you let Harvey know. It'll give me time to call Chris and my friend Rob at Snap Blocks. I need to make sure I protect my client. I need to tell everyone not to sign anything without talking to me first."

"An hour?" Sal confirmed.

"Yeah. Tell Harvey the guys at Snap Blocks had to cancel due to a personal emergency. My buddy Rob, who's my contact there, will cover if Harvey calls." Which he wouldn't because he liked to sit back on his ass. But Josh might call.

"Personal emergency," Sal murmured, like he was taking quick notes. "And don't forget you have a meeting at three with Sven about his second edition of Roadblocks, and before you ask, I'm still transcribing your notes from the calls you made last night. I'll share the file with you when I'm done."

"Great." I often recorded my calls and let Sal make sense of it later. "Let me know when everyone's present in the meeting at three."

"Will do."

"Thanks, Sal. I'll get back to you soon."

Blessing's deal was now top priority. She was leverage. It was time to formally introduce myself, so I could get my plans back on track.

She was going to be the catalyst of change. I would soon be in the driver's seat, steering the company exactly where it needed to go. It would be great again. I would see to that.

Blast Mendoza was going to be my lynchpin, but I needed to keep it in my pants.

This was going to be professional from here on out. This was going to be formal. I was going to tell her who I was, where I was from, and invite her to meet with me to see if we could make history with her game. We couldn't do that if I was more interested in knowing whether or not she was wearing panties.

But I knew she was. I knew what they looked like. God damn flowers on them. Some lace. Did she have others like that? Did she have a drawer with high octane sexy panties?

Shut up, Ian. Stop with this. It's your career, asshole.

No more underwear parties. No more clothing optional meet-ups. This was all going to be on the up-and-up.

I wanted to nurture a sense of confidence and trust with all my clients.

Blessing Mendoza was no different.

"Are you kidding me? He's a god damn pervert!"

And there was the siren's call.

Chapter 4
Ian

"Get him! Get him!"

It was like the universe was conspiring against me.

Her voice bled through the wall yet again, and even after having my job status threatened, and even as my logical brain was squaring away what needed to happen from here on out, my feet somehow made their own executive decision.

It was like she was an addiction.

I found myself in front of Blessing's still-shredded door for the second time in a day wondering how I was letting my personal interest in a woman come before business. It had never happened before.

"He's too fast!" an unfamiliar female voice cried out, followed by the sound of a door slamming.

came out crookedly anyway as she asked, "Are you all right?"

"Fantastic," I muttered, knowing I should let her go, but unable to loosen my arms from around her lower back. At least I hadn't grabbed her ass this time. Damn. She fit against me perfectly.

The heat pumped south yet again, making my cock feel heavier and fuller. Instantly. Definitely witchcraft. Sorcery. I focused in on her lips. They were a light pink. Free of make-up. Full. I had never wanted to taste a woman as much as I wanted to taste her.

"Holy fuck," she whispered. Her fingers tensed over my arms before spreading and sliding down my pecs in an involuntary-like caress, nails lightly rasping over my nipples, her eyes following greedily.

A low hiss of pleasure involuntarily escaped my lips, and now my hands both slid purposefully over her ass, cupping it, molding it. Hers was a gasp of pleasure before her lids grew weighted and she panted a light breath. It was a good look on her.

With her soft belly pressed against my hard cock that felt like I had a length of hot steel in my pants, and her eyes feasting on my chest, she breathed out, "Why do you have to be so hot? You have got to start wearing a damned shirt, Ian. We can't…I can't…I'm not even kidding. And maybe a jockstrap? Leash that monster! Please." Even as she said it, she was rubbing the monster with little movements of her hips, a quick, sweet grind that nearly had me coming in my pants.

What was it about this woman?

"This is all you," I muttered, a short chuckle rumbling from my chest. It took everything in me not to push the monster into her soft belly where he wanted to be properly stroked and appreciated. That would be the point of no return. But there was no way I could let go of her ass just yet. It felt too good in my hands, and I couldn't seem to care that it was not a good idea.

"I'm flattered." She looked back up at me with her snarky quirked lips again, but this time, there was a mischievous twist.

Her hands slid back up to my shoulders and into my hair. That goosebumps thing happened again, tripped up my neck and down over my body, causing me to suck in my breath. Hold it. Try to calm the gathering storm happening down south. One curious finger reached up, hooking around a stray lock that had fallen over my forehead, and pushed it back out of the way.

She whispered, "You look like you belong on a calendar spread."

"This is not helping the situation in my shorts," I murmured, after which she held my gaze and deliberately took a moment to rub her belly on my hard, needy cock yet again. It was getting to be a something other than how good she felt, how good she smelled, and how good she looked.

Was this something else I needed to apologize for?

When I saw that she was eyeing the monster tenting my shorts unashamedly, almost purring her appreciation, I figured not. Besides, she'd been teasing him. This was most definitely her fault. Maybe she needed to apologize to me because the monster was going to be denied, and it was going to take a while for him to chill the fuck out again.

She pulled away, and my hands felt so empty, I almost reached for her again. But I didn't. My reasoning skills were finally coming back online after getting short-circuited by her witchy, sorceress ways. I remembered I was supposed to be meeting with her professionally, not with the intent of bending her over a couch.

And even if we were interested in pursuing some fun, she deserved better than some kind of one-nighter. I did not do relationships. I couldn't. I refused to become my father. Period. I would not allow her to bewitch me any longer.

In any case, she'd already turned to face the dog again, so we didn't need to say anything else. The Kraken. He was standing on her bed, shaking with excitement that he'd finally gotten the humans to play with him.

"Come up on that side," she commanded,

stalking him on the far edge of the bed.

I made eye contact with the dog, coming to him swiftly. I wondered if what had worked before could work again. Scowling down at him, eyes locked on his, I commanded sharply, "Drop it."

His stub of a tail stopped wagging. His playful ears drooped, and his chin bowed with guilt. He dropped the scrap of cloth he'd had in his mouth into my waiting hand.

"Good boy," I patted his head, gave him a good scratch behind his ear, and he looked up at me with worshipful dark eyes. That's when I realized I was holding a lacy thong, now damp from dog drool. "He got to your panties?"

"Yes, because he's a perv," Blessing huffed, scrambling across the width of the bed on her knees to snatch them out of my hand.

Once again, despite my personal pep talk, some wild idea swept over me, and I held on to them, felt her soft skin on mine, sank into her eyes again when she looked up in question.

We were on the bed. I'd just been cupping her ass, an ass I'd already had the pleasure of seeing.

There was a breathless quality to her voice when she said, "He's a freaking Houdini Kraken— somehow got into my room, got them from my dirty clothes basket and decided to play with them."

Was it wrong that I didn't blame the dog? I could envision my own face between her thighs. They'd

There was a twinkle in her eye.

"Oh, I've checked him out plenty." I tried to keep my face casual, give a carefree smile. The blush was fighting to come back just thinking about him. What the hell was that about? Clearing my throat, I added, "He is definitely carrying. While it would be interesting to see if he, too, has a magic penis, I'm going to have to pass on that. He's too close to home."

"That's a rule? One you actually follow?" She mimed "mind blown" with her fingers by her temples.

"I know, right? But yes. You don't date neighbors, and you don't date at work for the same reason. You're going to see them every day, even when the magic wears off." But wouldn't it be worth it to jump in the sandbox and play with him for a little while? Play doctor? Maybe just for a little while? The kind of heat waves he'd been setting off in my body were seriously epic. What would it feel like to ride that wave to the end?

Okay. More pussy tingles. My body clearly liked the idea.

"But what if the magic doesn't wear off? What if you fall in love?"

I thought about that for a moment, then did something rare—I got real about my own issues.

Falling in love was my deepest fear.

"To be honest, I don't know if I have it in me to

love someone, you know?"

"Are you being serious?" Layla tilted her head. "But your parents."

"I know, I know. They have been seriously in love for more than forty years, yadda, yadda, yadda, but I can't help but wonder if I'm just built differently. Don't get me wrong. You know I have appreciated good dick here and there, but I'm like, almost harshly independent."

For good reason. There was so much more to this than I could say in a single session. And, it was something I'd chosen never to talk about. With anyone. See? Independent. I decided to keep to my casual explanation.

"My tolerance for male bullshit is like, nonexistent. No one has ever been that interesting for longer than a moon cycle, right? I've yet to meet a guy who genuinely saw me as more than a fuck toy."

Layla cocked her head. "But isn't that how you see them?"

"Maybe. It's just that I'm too used to doing whatever the fuck I want to do. I have big plans, and I don't want to get distracted by someone's magic penis."

Just then, feet pounded down the stairs before Mason, Layla's significant other, appeared in the archway across the room. As Layla's main-squeeze-stud-muffin, he was one of the few who had permission to enter at will during office hours.

His gray eyes searched for and found my friend in an instant. A sexy grin curled his lips, a look of love meant just for her, and maybe, for a moment, I was envious that I didn't have someone who looked at me like that. Did all happy couples have a look that was special to their partner? It seemed like my parents did, too.

That one look…it was a moment, a heartbeat, but it was so intimate, I had to look away. They spoke to each other without actually having to speak. What that was like, I didn't think I would ever know, and that made my heart give a little pang of protest. It just seemed that the men I'd met were all self-centered assholes, and even when I was with them, I was by myself.

I hadn't met anyone who wanted to know me. Really know me. But I couldn't say I blamed them. I was not typical. I was the weird kid in grade school who was always small, always interested in things no other girls could fathom, and always having to be scrappy to protect myself from the bullies.

My eyes burned. I blinked a few times.

Time to redirect myself again.

"Speaking of magic… Hi Mason!" I looked back up and winked at her.

It was my way of dispelling my own discomfort. Their intimacy was beautiful. Magical in a way because it was such an unknown quantity. Something I couldn't analyze. I couldn't problem solve it. It happened without some kind of instruction manual or handbook.

But how? Now I sounded like Jack Skellington trying to understand Christmas.

"Blessing!" Layla flushed even brighter, shaking her head at my use of the word "magic."

"How's it going?" Mason nodded with a more subdued smile, leaning against the side of the arch. He was big and sexy. Ex-military turned business owner. Layla had already pushed out of her chair to join him.

"Well," I sighed, giving his question serious consideration, "I have two teenage boys for the week, and I'm supposed to create a structured environment for them to live in as they do their very best to create chaos, while at the same time, trying to get my own shit done. So, doing peachy."

"Sounds like fun," Mason's grin widened, but it was mainly because Layla had swooped in to plant a quick kiss on his neck, the part of his body she was able to reach without jumping. Very cute. He was restraining himself from pushing her up against the wall. I could tell. It was like his eyes were compelled to remain on her face. Bewitched.

That was an interesting idea. Bewitching someone. Enchanting them. Making them only see you. How would one go about that? Thinking about it for the game of course. It might be an interesting aspect to bring to *Multiverse Infinity*.

Bring an elixir. A spell book from the ancient druids that would require multiple quests to first understand the symbols and language? To be able to enchant, one would have to give time, energy, and attention to the task of understanding the culture of the druids or witches or …whatever I wanted to call them.

Not because I wanted a guy like Mason. Not like I needed a guy like Hulk. I mean, Ian. I didn't need someone to be smitten. Right? No. Yeah? What? Of course not. Definitely not.

"Hey, who's that?" Mason asked, noting the large dog who'd finally decided to crash at my feet.

"Part of the chaos."

It was a strange thing. After feeding him, walking him, cleaning up after him and bringing him back to the apartment, he'd stuck by my side everywhere I went. To the kitchen, where I may or may not have dropped some tidbits from my lunch—to the office, where I worked through developing a complex forest maze with portals for one of my game levels, and to the entertainment area (now with a new door) where he settled with his head over my feet while I looked up the game Pedro had recommended. Downloaded it.

The Kraken had also insisted on laying on the tiles by the door when I showered late in the afternoon after doing some yoga using the new fitness app I'd discovered. But that wasn't the strange part. What was strange was that I didn't mind this new shadow.

His enormous head was resting on my feet, so they'd long ago gone numb, but he'd been sleeping so peacefully, I hadn't wanted to disturb him by moving them. Blood flow was overrated anyway, right?

Hearing Mason, though, he'd popped his head up, his ears cocked. All right. He was cute. Maybe. Even if he'd left drool on me. If I didn't think about it too much, it wouldn't gross me out.

"Blessing's nephews brought him last night," Layla grinned up at him. As though unable to help himself, he wrapped both arms around her, and dipped his head to lay one on her. Brief, but powerful, based on Layla's dazed look when he pulled back. Satisfied with how he left her, he looked down at the dog again.

"He's a big boy. What's his name?" Mason asked, still not releasing Layla, like he couldn't get enough of just holding her.

"I'm calling him Kraken until my nephews come home and explain where they got him from."

"Where they got him from?" He looked confused. Him and me both.

"According to my sister, they are never going to have a dog. The boys know this. My brother-in-law is allergic. Which I didn't know. Or I would have had more questions for them."

"They were hoping," Mason squeezed on Layla a little tighter before planting a kiss on top of her head and pulling back to look down at her. "Ready to go or do you need more time?"

It was nearing five, and we'd been chit-chatting for the last hour besides. It was time for her to fly. Be free. Get another dose of magic penis.

"My stuff is done. I'm ready now. Speaking of hope, uh…Sweetheart?" Layla had finally recovered from the kiss and looked up at him with a bright smile. Overly bright. Mesmerizingly bright. Was this part of the enchanting process? Layla cocked her head playfully and said, "I have a question for you."

He heard the tone, saw the smile on her face and gave a suspicious look. "What?"

"I was just talking to Bethany earlier, and we had a good conversation."

Hmmm. The she-devil who'd tried to break them up just a few weeks back. This was the first I'd heard of this. Since when had she decided to "Good Witch" the enemy? Bet, as she was sometimes called, was a bitch of the first degree.

"And?" Mason asked, unsuccessfully fighting his scowl. He was still feeling the burn of it all, clearly.

"Yeah, well, I convinced her to move home. Stay with her mom to save money, you know," Layla rubbed at his pec, still facing him in a loosened hug.

"Okay. That's good?" He was guessing, by his tone.

"It is, right? It is good. Really good. A step in the right direction, wouldn't you say?"

He gave up on following her circuitous questions. "Tell me your question."

"Well, she needs a job while she tries to figure out what she's going to do."

He straight on scowled. "I see where this is going. No way."

"She is up for anything."

"I'm not working with her."

"See, you wouldn't have to. Right? Schedule her for time at the club when you're not going to be there." She looked so earnest. I could see the slow resignation on his face. So could Layla, which was why she continued. "She's really not a bad person. Actually, she sent me an apology for her behavior and said that she knew you were the absolute best and was glad you seemed happy. It seemed really heartfelt. And I'm not asking for her. She doesn't know I'm talking with you."

"I think we're going to need to discuss this," he exhaled a heavy breath, but it was the sound of a man acknowledging defeat. He was going to give in. Even I could see it.

"Of course. On the ride home?"

"Yeah. All right," he grunted, squinting down at

her as though the idea pained him. She dodged back to her desk to gather her stuff, flashing her brilliant smile at him again. "You won't regret this. Sometimes, people just need help. Right?"

Oh, that was sneaky of her. She'd needed that help a few years ago when she was escaping an abusive relationship, and I'd helped, which had then allowed her to be with Mason.

"Layla," he grumbled, "all I said was that we should talk about this."

"I know, but…"

There was a sudden ruckus coming through the door on the third floor. Kraken jumped up, looked toward where the noise was coming from, identified the familiar tone of the voices jabbing at each other, and then set his tail to wagging a mile a minute. His playmates were back.

"Hey, Blessing!" Cody hollered.

"We're home," Finn called out immediately after.

The sound of them pounding down the stairs was followed by their appearance near Mason, coming through the other side of the rounded entryway. I gave them an arch look.

"What did I tell you to call me?"

For a moment, they both looked confused before Finn gave a wide grin. He elbowed his brother and said, "Oh, right. Ruler of the Queendom."

"Thank you."

My identical nephews were younger versions of Jason Mamoa, which made sense since their dad was also part Hawaiian. They had his size and the Mendoza cloud-blue eyes. Being that they were only ten years younger than me, they left off the Aunt title. It felt more like I was their big sister, besides. Kraken launched himself at them, whole butt wagging, long tongue licking, and rapid-fire pawing at them excitedly.

"Speaking of the spawn of Satan," I arched a brow casually. "These are my nephews, Cody and Finn."

"No, I'm Cody," one of them said, a devilish twinkle in his eye before bending to scratch Kraken's head.

On cue, his brother offered, "And I'm Finn."

I wasn't fazed. They fucked with me all the time, but I knew what to look for. "Bullshit. Anyway, you know Layla, and this is her man, Mason," I pointed out everyone in the room before pointing to the overly large wiggling creature in the room. "And now you can tell me who this is and where you got him from."

"And that's our cue to leave. I think you guys are going to need to talk," Mason nodded to all, offering a fist bump to the boys as they passed through the archway.

They returned the gesture, but Cody squinted at him. "Hey, man. I know you. I've seen you on the waves. You can shred."

Mason nodded and did that guy-smirk thing. "Yeah. Thanks. Mornings, usually. Best time."

"Cool. Maybe we'll see you out there."

Mason gave a friendly salute while pulling Layla back through the archway toward the stairs. "For sure, guys. Catch you later."

I squinted up at them from my desk. "You aren't getting out of this. Where did you get the dog?"

"What do you mean? He's our dog," Finn insisted, kneeling to finally give Kraken a full body scratch that launched him straight into doggie heaven. On his back. Legs in the air. Offering better access to his belly.

"Not according to your mom."

"You called mom?" Cody frowned, his devilish twinkle turning into a look of concern. "Was she pissed?"

"She's in Hawaii staring at the ocean. What do you think?" I leaned back in my chair. "So where did you get him?"

The boys looked at each other before Finn spoke up. "There was a homeless guy sitting on the corner. Said he got kicked out of his house a month ago and couldn't afford to feed the dog anymore. That's why he's so skinny."

"He just gave you the dog."

"Yup. We were about to come up here last night and stopped for a sec to give him a pat." Finn took a moment to accept the sudden barrage of doggie licks to his face. I tried not to be grossed out by that. "The cops were out moving the homeless guys off the beach, and this guy was afraid his dog would end up getting killed in a shelter because he's a Rottweiler and not everyone wants one."

Cody straightened up again. "He said most people are afraid of big dogs, and he didn't want to see that happen to his little buddy."

"Little buddy?" I scoffed, pushing out of my chair and heading toward the stairs to go back up to my pad on the third floor. Kraken noted I was on the move and excitedly ran ahead of us. He knocked into me in the process, beating us to the stairs like it was a race, almost knocking me down. I grabbed the railing to keep upright. "Yeah, right. Little."

"You're not going to take him to a shelter are you, Bless?" Finn had a worried look pinching his brows together.

On a sigh, I followed poochy-pooch upstairs. "I don't know what I'm going to do. Why did you bring me a dog when I am not an animal person? You really didn't think this through."

"You wouldn't want them to kill him." Finn offered again, selling this as hard as he could.

Cody turned his sad eyes on me, pausing halfway up the stairs to look back at me. "What would you have done?"

They were good. I had to give them that.

"I don't know. I don't chat with homeless people, usually." I barely got out of the house to go grocery shopping. Hence my empty fridge. Also, my next problem to solve. I supposed my nephews would need to eat soon, and a lot. They were big, growing boys. At this point, I actually had more dog food in the apartment than people food.

Cody continued up the stairs.

"He's a cool dog, don't you think?" Finn trudged up the stairs behind his brother.

"He's freaking expensive, is what he is. I bought him all this dog stuff. Fed him. Walked him. We don't even know if he has all his shots. Probably not since he was on the streets, and that will be another bunch of money." We came up to the third floor, and I headed toward the entertainment area where I flopped down on the couch.

They each took a different part of the U-shaped sectional. Their jackets, skateboards, and backpacks were now dumped in the middle of the kitchen. The kitchen with very little food in it. Hmmm. What to do.

Kraken joined us. Sat on my feet again. Watched me. He was cute. For sure.

"I need to think more about this hellhound situation, but I promise not to do anything without letting you guys know."

Kraken was sitting so pretty, waiting for a clue. I didn't have one. His soft brown eyes were melting with unconditional love as they watched me. I gave a mental shrug and sighed. It was too much to think about now.

"Pizza okay?" I asked, looking at the time. Dinner was a few hours off, but at least I could have a plan in motion. "What should I get? Large? Pepperoni? You aren't into any weird flavors, right?"

"Yeah, well, we were going to hit the break and then grab some food with friends," Cody offered slowly, giving me a side-eye as he spoke. Analyzing the landscape.

"Nuh-uh. Nice try. Your mom said you could surf, but then you had to be home by seven. It's a school night, and you have finals starting Wednesday. And, before you head out, you need to feed the Kraken, and take him for a walk again."

"Aww!" Finn grouched.

"Hey, you brought him. You took responsibility for him. Now you have to help until we figure out what to do."

"You used to be fun," Cody muttered.

"Oh, I'm fun. I am a laugh riot. A barrel of monkeys. An aunt who takes care of a rando homeless man's dog that her nephews spontaneously sprang on her. An aunt who has all the coolest new video games that they get the chance to play when they are all finished with their work tonight. Well, unless I'm not fun anymore."

A grin snuck through when Cody admitted, "Okay. You're still fun."

"Excellent. In fact, come check out the new game I downloaded. I have it on good authority that it's hella cool."

"Blessing?"

"Yes?"

"No one says 'hella' anymore."

"Which makes it even more cool when I do because vintage always comes back in style."

Chapter 6
Ian

"So, you're a stalker now?" Through my headset, I heard Pedro's amusement.

It made me want to clock him.

I scowled at my monitor, in the grips of an edgy aggravation that had me revved. It didn't help that Pedro was trying to wreck me on GTA. Wasn't this supposed to be a friendly goddamn game of Grand Theft Auto?

We were talking on the headsets as we played online for a few minutes during lunch, but he'd managed to kill me off three times already.

Asshole.

And I wasn't fucking stalking her.

This wasn't stalking.

I was not stalking my little blonde bombshell Blast.

It just so happened that I saw this place was up for sale, and it was a good deal. Sound investment. There was no new coastline being made in California. The property value would only rise, not fall, over time. This wasn't the only investment property I had.

This is what I'd told myself, even though none of this made sense.

My personal finance manager was not opposed to this purchase, not that he'd fully understood it.

"You know there are actual beach front properties you could buy in the same area?" he'd offered, confusion lining his forehead. I didn't explain. Just told him to make it happen.

She'd called me her Hulk.

Fuck.

I'd never before found myself in this position.

The idea of being her personal superhero, her bodyguard, the guy who was allowed to grab her ass to help her grind on me, was only adding to my need to be around her. How could she become an obsession overnight? How many times had I relived the slow grind she'd been doing on my dick?

Countless. That's how many.

Why was I not surprised that on top of everything else I'd experienced, our own chemistry, the chemistry between us, was explosive? Everything with her was novel, including the way I'd first become aware of her. There was no one else who had ever grabbed my attention in a strangle hold.

And she had no idea she'd done that long before I'd even laid eyes on her in person.

She'd inspired me. Reawakened a significant part of me that I'd thought was long dead. She'd done that. Because of her, I'd looked back ten years to a time when I had still wanted a particular future for myself, before reality interceded, forcing me toward a different life path.

But how could I explain all this when I barely understood it myself? She was the origin of my Glitch. Blessing Blast Mendoza.

So, this was not being a stalker. Her work was off-the-charts amazing. It was no bullshit that I wanted to offer her an opportunity. She could find herself leveling up in a way she couldn't even prepare for. The money she could earn would make her head spin.

This was also what I was telling myself.

Where the hell was she, anyway? It was past the lunch hour already. She always came out on the patio at lunch. I fought off the growl trapped in my chest.

I hadn't caught sight of Blessing in more than twenty-four hours now. Business had taken over, as usual—video conferencing the meetings of the day, phone calls to all my people with a warning of potential shadiness from the company heading their way. It had eaten up the rest of my day yesterday and most of the day so far today.

But I kept listening for sounds of her movement, an echo of her soft voice through the wall that was usually saying something outrageous or snarky. Watching for a glimpse of her was now my new hobby. It was making me nuts. There were two issues here, really.

First off, I wanted this gorgeous girl. She was perfect for me. I needed to fuck her in the worst way. Grab hold of her ass and pound my dick into her until we were both coming hard. My cock jerked with that thought.

Second, she was my inspiration, and I was afraid of losing that feeling again. It was fragile. Without proper attention and nourishment, I would once again find myself in the cold void of business, where only the numbers seemed to matter.

It felt like I had only a short window in which to see. But see what? I wasn't sure. It wasn't like I'd planned to stop working. I was Ian Patrick of the gaming world. But I was driven to this point through gut instinct, and I always listened to my gut.

But neither did I have the time for any of it. Hence, aggravation. Frustration. There had never been a time where I didn't know what to do, what my next step needed to be. I'd made necessary choices, and they had always driven the bus.

Which was why I could not do relationships.

I was always working, traveling, scouting. Making a solid commitment would be impossible. I would never allow myself to make promises that I knew I could not keep. There would never be a time that I would fuck someone over. I refused to be like my father. Ever.

There could be no relationship, and Blast deserved everything that I couldn't give her. Why couldn't I remember that when we were together?

Because the thought of some other asshole touching her, being close to her, instantly pissed me off.

I wondered what she was doing now. If she was eventually going to come out on the patio where I could see her. What could she be wearing that would make me crazy? What would I want her to wear? Bikini Princess Leia. Absolutely. Wasn't that every man's fantasy?

Too cold, though. The usual marine layer was creating a gray sky. She shouldn't come out wearing that.

Unless it was just the two of us. At her place.

Pedro killed me again.

"What the fuck," I growled. "Seriously?"

"I could do this all day," he laughed outright. "Your mind is on her."

"Only because I need to introduce myself formally. Let her know the company is interested."

"And you needed to move? To make an immediate, life-altering move to Hermosa Beach to do that? There is this not-so-radically-new invention called an airplane. Right? The idea being that you fly somewhere, stay at a hotel, and...wait for it...fly back home when your business is done."

"Fuck off," I muttered. "I still have my place up in the Bay Area. I didn't get rid of it."

But it was like I had this fever. The more I'd been exposed to her, been around her, the more I needed to see her. I was burning to see her.

And yes, I wanted to rub on her, too. Immerse myself in her. Unfortunate side effect.

"Whatever you need to tell yourself. It's still a stalker move to buy the place next to her."

"It's not stalking." Modulating my tone, I said calmly, "You're the asshole who told me about Hermosa Beach over the last ten years. I was already interested in checking it out."

"You do nothing for the last ten years, but suddenly, you're going to up and move next door to her once you've seen what she's about? That's called stalking."

"It was serendipity." In a sense, it was.

She'd blindsided me, first by the game model Pedro had shown me that he was working on with her, and then by stories of her, images of her. Her eyes had the ability to grab you, like there was a secret dancing on the air that she wanted to share.

If I could work through this with her, figure out what I needed to learn here, my life could get back to normal.

That was the real reason I was living next door to her.

I'd visited him while on a business trip to the Netherlands, and the cell door to my creative mind, secured shut for so many years, had finally been unlocked. I'd spent hours, the entire night, checking out everything he'd had that was related to the game, even after Pedro had passed out from exhaustion. I'd riddled him with questions, not only about the game, but about the game maker, learning everything I could.

I was awake the entire night.

Her work had ideas flooding my brain, had my adrenaline pumping on high. Possibilities. Potential futures. Her game had empires built upon empires with crazy steampunk-influenced magic interwoven that begged to be lived in. Explored. There were discoveries to be made. From the first moment, she hadn't left my mind. The story had webbed through my brain, unfinished.

Captivating. All of it.

I had to know everything about her.

I'd found snapshots on his corkboard above his electronics charging station. Intermixed with "to do" lists, random stickers, inspirational quotes, and messages from others, carelessly pinned there with

metal pins, were a series of old snapshots. I'd
memorized them while he'd snored like a
hibernating bear, sprawled across his couch.

One image was of the two of them clowning
around at some computer camp over a summer in
elementary school. She wasn't wearing her glasses
yet. Her white-blonde hair was braided in pigtails.
Her smile was as wide as her excited, pale blue
eyes.

Another picture, a little older, was on the beach.
Middle school? Maybe. Wetsuits. Boogie boards
held aloft with silly grins and hair plastered to their
heads like they'd just exited the water. Pedro was
getting taller in this picture. She was still her petite
self. Still not wearing her glasses. Despite her size,
she was larger than life, even then. Staring down the
camera with the smirk I was beginning to recognize.
Somehow, she just looked in charge of the situation.

Then there was the high school one. Kissing his
cheek at their high school graduation. Pedro had hit
six feet by then. She looked to be almost a foot
shorter. There were the glasses. Perched on her
nose. Fucking adorable. Which reminded me of the
question I'd been wanting to ask. I asked it now.

"Did you guys date in high school?"

"Me and B-girl? No. Why?"

"No reason." But there was clearly a sense of
relief in my gut. An unclenching. The idea that
they'd maybe been close and personal, maybe

fucked, had been eating at me. Not outright. Just enough to be like a constant thorn. An annoying idea that I'd needed to clear up.

"I'm telling you; you like her. I can tell."

"Clearly, she's hot, but I don't get personal with people I want to work with."

"Bullshit. Listen to me, punk. Don't hurt her. Don't just fuck around with her. She deserves better than that." Normally laid back, Pedro's voice was suddenly fierce.

"I'm not going to hurt her. I'm not going to do anything." My voice felt like a rough patch of road, barely audible as I contained my anger because I'd gone through this argument in my own head.

"No, really. I'm serious. You want to know how we met? I'll tell you. I was getting bullied in the second grade. Some kids were making fun of me because I still had an accent. She came out of nowhere and shoved her way through the group with this crazy-sounding battle cry. She gave no warning. Just bonzai'ed into the group of boys and opened a fucking can of whoop-ass all over them.

"And she was this little fucking kid. Not bigger than me. I promise. And she was swinging haymakers with her little fists, power throwing them toward the goddamn ceiling to get these boys away from me. She actually managed to make one of the kids cry when she clocked him in the face. Then she tells them that she'll follow them home and beat them all up again if they don't leave me alone. I didn't know what the fuck to do. I wasn't sure if I should be scared of her myself."

Of course she did that. I could totally see that about her. Unapologetic. Bigger than life.

A feeling of pride warmed my insides. Why, I didn't know. It's not like I had anything to do with who she was or what she did. But she struck me as a ride or die kind of friend. Those were rare in my life. There were a lot of bullshit people in my world. I wanted more of her kind.

Ride or die loyalty. I could count on three fingers the number of people I had like that: My mom, my assistant, and Pedro. Small circle.

"That's how you became friends?"

"Yeah." He chuckled after a moment. "She told me I was going to be Spiderman, and she was going to be Batman, and that our job was to watch out for the bad guys. Batman, Ian. She was badass from birth. So that's what we did. If there was ever an injustice happening on the playground, we were there to resolve it.

"She saved me, Ian. Who knows what I would be doing now if not for her. Helped me learn better English. Taught me how to read using those damned comics of hers, forcing me to because she told me I needed to learn how to act like spiderman. So of course, I did it. For her."

Even bigger. Again, she was…more.

"You have created a shitstorm, Ian," Pedro growled quietly through my earbuds on the talk app we were using. "You need to come clean, man."

"I plan to." As if on cue, I heard the sound of her door opening.

She was about to come out.

Chapter 7
Ian

Blessing appeared on the roof patio alone, directly in my line of sight.

She dropped into a chair at the small teak table. It was not a coincidence that I'd temporarily set up my workplace on the dining table where I had full view of her. She was looking up at the sky, catching a few of the sun's rays that had broken through the clouds.

Wasn't she cold? It was December at the beach. It was like sixty degrees outside.

She needed a jacket. Didn't that costume have a black trench coat that went with it? Pretty sure it was a signature Trinity item. Seriously. I was tempted to go outside and drape a sweatshirt over her shoulders. Besides, there was some part of me that liked the idea of her being draped in something of mine.

The idea had warmth seeping through my chest.

Layla was nowhere to be seen. Kraken appeared, his large body trying to squeeze into the impossibly small space under the table, plopping himself down at Blessing's feet. He dropped his head over them in a sign of devotion while he settled in to snooze.

Somehow, I was beginning to understand the sentiment.

He was a good dog.

Fuck. What was I doing with her? I still had her panties. Her silky little panties.

Heat cruised through my cock, and I had to reach down to readjust myself in my pants.

It had been a bad idea. I knew this. Why did I take her panties? And did I need to give them back?

The answer, clearly, was that I was overcome with the desire to fuck her, and I was not giving them back. Simple. Stupid, though. I knew it.

Today, she was in her Trinity costume from The Matrix. All black. Black boots and shiny black pants and tank that were fitted. Her blond hair was up in a bun with two sticks holding it up, leaving her neck, jawline, and shoulders clearly visible. Elegant.

Nibbling that skin popped into mind. She smelled so good, and she was so soft.

Black shades completed the look. Had to be prescription. For a moment, I worried. She wouldn't sacrifice safety for a costume, would she?

"I told you she wanted no part of you," Pedro continued, breaking into my thoughts by virtually smashing into my ride again for emphasis in our video game. "Gamecon is the evil empire."

It pissed me off to hear him say that again. "Yes, I got that the first and second time you mentioned it. I haven't talked to her yet, but I plan to."

"Today."

"Today," I confirmed, sounding more certain than I was feeling.

I had no idea how I was going to do this.

Maybe bringing dinner later was the way to go. Feed the troops, wait for them to get busy with their homework or gaming or whatever kids did these days after school. It would be easy enough to explain. Reasonable that I didn't tell her who I was during our underwear romp the day before.

"She's going to be pissed. Maybe at both of us."

"You told her Gamecon was interested. She can't get mad at you, and it's not like you knew I was moving to a new pad next door to her. Besides, this also brings me closer to my mom."

Even I knew it was a stretch, so it didn't surprise me that Pedro snorted in reaction.

I narrowed my eyes on the monitor, had my character take out my own anxiety on the innocent bystander in the video game by throwing him off his motorcycle and jacking it from him. It was, after all, the point of the game.

"Doesn't she live in Bakersfield? How is moving to Hermosa closer to her? You'll still need a whole day to go hang out. It's not exactly right next door. So, like I said before, you like her, and now you'll have to explain to her why you moved next door. Hence, stalker."

"Fuck you." But my voice was calm as I said it.

"Frankly, I think you're fucked, but you're welcome to get a second opinion."

There had been no plan to move until I'd seen the other unit for sale in her building, while I'd been virtually snooping. Googled her specs toward the early dawn that momentous day while making a fresh pot of coffee. Arranged a virtual tour of the space and knew I had to have it. Had to be there. Close to her. Grabbed the offer without letting myself think on it too much.

"Make sure she knows I had nothing to do with this. Nothing. You did not tell me what you were doing the last time you were in town."

"I will. Honestly, I surprised myself." And Pedro was right. I was fucked.

Blessing stood up from her chair, and I waited to see what pose she would give me today. Bent over the table again? That was my favorite. It made me envision being behind her. I could take those sticks out of her hair, mess her up a bit. Or maybe she would be blowing kisses this time?

She didn't do either.

She walked out toward the edge of the patio to look over the rooftops toward the ocean. It was a gray day, the mist still hanging off the clouds.

She rubbed at her arms. She was cold.

I exhaled, not even realizing I'd been holding my breath.

"And I'm going to call her tomorrow to make sure she knows who the stalker is taking up residence next door, so get on it," Pedro warned. "I swear it. I'm not fucking around with this. She and I have always had each other's backs, and just because it's you doesn't mean I won't warn her."

"Tonight," I repeated absently, still watching her.

"Oh, and dude? You're dead. Again."

My gaze snapped back to my computer screen where I had, in fact, driven at full speed off the cliff into the beautiful blue ocean. Crash and burn. I hoped that was not an omen.

"It's getting late here," Pedro said on what sounded like a yawn. "I'm going to grab some food and chill for a few before bed."

"Have a good one."

And then I couldn't take the distance any longer.

Before I'd given it much thought, I found myself at the patio doors, my hand pushing the slider out of the way. I'd made it so the entire wall could open up, making it an indoor/outdoor experience from my side of the unit. She didn't move, even though I knew she'd heard me.

Kraken came up to me, tail wagging. I gave him a rough scratch behind the ears before he went back to his spot under the table, watching us.

It felt too natural at this point to walk up behind her, blanket her with my own body to block the cool air, let my hands run down her chilled arms to warm them. She leaned back into me.

"Do you need my sweatshirt?"

"You would take it off and give it to me?"

"In a heartbeat."

"Why would I need it when I have you? You seem to be missing someone, though," she said, a hint of a sultry tone, and gave me a side glance, but her glasses were too dark. It bothered me that I couldn't see her eyes. She had beautiful eyes.

"Who is that?" I asked, bending so my lips were near her ear with my whiskers tickling her skin. I wasn't sure where she was going with that statement, but I was more interested in the sight of her nipples hardening under her black tank. I had a perfect line of sight over her shoulder and a fantasy of pulling her shirt up so my fingers could have at them.

In answer, she wriggled her ass against my cock. The monster responded instantly. Getting thicker. Heavier.

"Ah. There he is," she smirked. "I like having him around."

"He's shy," I murmured.

"Not from my experience," she responded, a bit breathier.

"He likes to come out to play when he's invited to."

"He needs an invitation?" She swayed her hips back and forth, rubbing her perfect ass against my shaft. My hands went to her hips to stay them, but just like before, I only ended up helping her grind just right. The monster erection was roaring to life behind the button fly of my jeans. It was startling how quickly she could have me pulsing with the need to be inside her. "Like that?"

"Exactly," I whispered in her ear. Her breath caught on a barely detectable whimper.

"You still have my panties," she said in a shaky voice.

"I do." I'd rubbed them over my hard cock last night, thinking about what it would feel like to stuff her with it. The monster. Then I'd rubbed one out in the shower thinking about it.

"Has he come out to play with them? They're silky soft."

"He's a gentleman. He doesn't kiss and tell."

"He's a gentleman? Ha!" She let her hands wander up behind her head to where they were barely able to latch behind my neck. Her tits were pushed out. Begging to be touched. My fingers moved up her ribcage, stopping just short of her lush mounds. She felt so delicate under my big hands. There was an urge to bend her to my will. It was hot. Primal.

It would have been so easy to keep going until they were covering her breasts, cupping them. Playing with them until she was moaning for more. Sliding a hand into her pants to see how slick she was with arousal…

Fuck, it was hard to think.

She smelled so good. I wanted to take those damn sticks out of her hair. Wrap my fingers in her soft blonde mane.

"So what do you do all day, my Hulk?"

That was just the question she needed to ask to get me out of my lust-filled headspace. A deep breath helped to get my thoughts straight. I needed to talk to her. Tell her who I was. Set up a meeting. Formally. But here we were. Again. Chemistry that was ready to explode getting volleyed between us. It was dangerous.

I paused. This was it. The moment to come clean. My fingers tensed on her narrow ribcage.

"Well, Blast, I do tech. It lets me work from home or wherever."

"'Blast'? Hmmm. I like it. Blast and Hulk. A new superhero duo. My superhero power would have to be blowing shit up, right?"

"Oh, yeah," I agreed, thinking about just how much my life was blown up because of her.

"What kind of tech?" she asked, letting her fingernails scrape lightly over my scalp while tossing another look at me to acknowledge her new pet name. I fought against the pleasure of her touch. A shiver went down my spine.

Taking a deep breath, I confessed, "Gaming."

"Really?" She suddenly whirled to face me, and I missed the feel of her hands in my hair. Her platinum brows arched above the frame of her sunglasses. She sounded excited. "Are you a gamer? What do you play? What are you into?"

"RPGs, mostly, but I like other stuff."

"Really? What role playing games are you into?"

And here was the moment. This could go bad fast. I opened my mouth to respond, and my phone rang.

It was the ringtone I used for my mom. Every time I heard it, there was an immediate twinge of panic, even after all this time.

I looked at Blessing as I pulled it out of my pocket. "I need to get this."

"No problem. Come over when you're done if you have a moment. My friend turned me on to a cool game. I'm hooked. I think you're going to love it." She did a quick wave of her fingers, and I watched the swing of her ass as she disappeared back inside her door. She left it open. For me. I was being welcomed in.

Swiping to answer, I said, "Mom. Is everything

all right?"

"As right as it can be when you're my age. Did you get moved in, sweetheart?"

"For the most part." I was glad she sounded good. Healthy. Stronger. "I still have some boxes that'll show up in the next few days, and the final renovation work will get done by the end of the week, so I'm all set."

"I'm glad you moved down, sweetheart. I'd like to be able to see you more."

"I know I'm not real close," I said, thinking of my conversation with Pedro, "but Mom—"

"You're closer than you were, and that's wonderful. It would be silly for you to move back here. I would be mad at you if you did. I'm not sick anymore," she said with some exasperation. "Tell me how things are going. How's work?"

"It's good." I went back inside my apartment to have this conversation. Every day with my mother alive was a gift. I'd learned that lesson the hard way.

"Anything new you're chasing after?"

Blessing's playful smirk came to mind. But was I *chasing* her? I hesitated a moment, reluctant to answer, but this was my mom. We'd been a team for a long time, and on some level, I wanted her to know about Blessing.

"There's a new game I'm after. It's unexpected. It'll makes waves, mom. I can't wait to see the full

scope of it. Maybe have a part in bringing it to life."
I thought about the woman next door. Blast. Hulk
and Blast. It made me smile. She made me smile. It
was yet another part of my life she'd changed.

"What's the name of it?"

"So you can play it when it comes out?" I teased.
My mother was not into playing games. She much
preferred watching her reality TV shows with her
friends.

"Smartass," she chided, but I could hear the
smile on her end.

"It's called *Multiverse Infinity.* The woman who
created the game is kind of...surprising."

"A woman? I don't think you've had a woman
on your design team. At least not one you've talked
about."

"Not many, but there are a few on my team."

"What makes this one so special?"

"She's unusual, quirky, but in the best way.
Gorgeous. Smart. Funny. She worked her ass off on
this game, spent years on it. Laid it all out there. I'm
hoping to officially ask her to join up with us. It's
beautiful. The kind of stuff I hoped I would create
when I was younger."

"You still could, you know. Nothing's stopping
you," she interjected softly.

"I'm pretty sure that ship's sailed."

"It doesn't have to stay that way. This job isn't
what you wanted."

"I was glad to do this, mom. You know that."

"I know, I know. You took care of me. You did what you needed to do to pay the bills. Breast cancer with no medical insurance is usually a death sentence. I can't tell you how sorry I am that you had to face that decision, but you don't have to anymore."

"If all goes as planned, I'll be taking over the reins of the company."

"But you don't need the money anymore, sweetheart. You can finally take the time to do what you want to do."

The pull to do just that was strong, but so was the anxiety. I'd been in this life for too long, and I needed it. I needed to be ready. For what, I wasn't sure. "It's what I do mom. It's how I live."

"It's scary to start over, but if anyone can do it, you can. Face this demon, Ian. I'm healthy. You have more money than you could spend in a lifetime, and now you need to start enjoying life. You have earned it."

"I'm enjoying what I do. I promise." The idea of not having the high-powered job that kept me running wasn't something I was willing to embrace. Fear of the cancer returning, of not having this one thing that I could control, that would help pay for any treatment under the sun, was the kind of PTSD I was dealing with. It almost felt like I would be inviting that phone call that told me she was near death again if I stopped doing this kind of work. Every day I thanked the fucking stars and planets and whoever else might be out there that she was alive. It still made me ill to remember what she'd looked like while going through chemo.

There was no way in hell I could ever give up this job. It was laughable to think that way. If not this company, there were others that would beg me to join them, and I could name my price. I was worth my weight in gold. I'd proven that.

"I worry about you, Ian."

"Don't worry about me. I'm good. Especially if she takes my meeting. I'm hoping to plead my case tonight."

"Oh! That's soon. Where is this girl? Don't tell me you have to travel again already. I hate that you're always having to go here and there and here."

"Not at all. She lives right next door." The moment the words came out, I realized what I'd revealed. My mother grew quiet.

After a few moments, she said, "I'm going to pray that you get exactly what you truly want."

"We'll see what happens. I'll let you know. Anyway, I don't see why you won't let me move you out to the beach. I've got plenty of room here, and it's beautiful," I stated, looking out the window toward the ocean.

"You have your life. Maybe I can come visit

here and there, but you don't need to be living with your mother again. Besides, I'm living my best life in my favorite home with my best friends. You made that happen. Be happy for me. I beat cancer."

I smiled, thinking of how I'd gone overboard after becoming flush. I'd sent my mother on a cruise to Hawaii with her two best friends, once she was in remission. While she was gone, I'd refurbished her house. I didn't want her living in a shithole, especially since she was insistent on remaining there.

"All right, mom. Is there anything else you need?"

"No, I'm good."

"Let's talk soon. I love you, mom."

"Love you too, sweetheart."

She no longer had to work. She might refuse to leave the small house she'd lived in all my life, but she didn't have to work, and the house had been upgraded. She'd been a house cleaner, barely making ends meet when I was growing up. Now she was a lady of the house.

Now she could finally relax.

Blessing had left her sliding door open. Entering, I found her lounging on her couch with her feet kicked up on the coffee table, Kraken under her legs again. Her sunglasses had been switched out for her regular ones. I was glad, because one of the best things about her was her expressive eyes. I loved seeing the snark, the dry humor swirling around in their pale blue depths.

She had a game controller in her lap and was staring intently at the television. Looking up at the screen, it took a moment for me to recognize the game—and then the air got sucked out of the room. For a moment, I couldn't breathe, only stare.

"Have you seen this one?" she asked, working the buttons. "My friend hooked me onto this one yesterday. Ended up playing it for hours. I got no work done last night. I was hunting for supplies to protect this town I'd built until I was cross-eyed, and that's saying something. I was fighting off scavengers that tried to raid us. Totally addicting. It's called—"

"Terminus," I interrupted, sensing a strange, fated, out of reality moment happening. Goosebumps tripped up my arms. Especially after the conversation with my mother.

"Yeah! You know it?"

A sudden surge of surprise and pleasure mixed together in my blood stream. It pumped like a drug through my body. I couldn't believe what I was seeing. Someone was playing my game. Not just someone. She was. Blessing was. And she liked it.

It felt so personal. The game was the errant child I'd had to give up on long ago, but that didn't mean I didn't still love it. It was an extension of me. The deepest part of me from long ago. And she liked it.

"You've played it?" She was still working the controls. "It's good, right?"

"Yeah, I played it. A lot. Actually, I designed it."

The play was paused. There was a beat of silence. Then she turned to look at me like she needed clarification. Her eyebrows arched almost comically above her glasses.

"What was that?"

"It's my game."

"You created this? Made this game? Did the actual design? You did?"

She rocketed the questions at me, like maybe I wasn't understanding exactly what she was asking.

"Yeah. I did the coding, too. I worked on it when I was an undergrad and in grad school. Back when I had some extra time."

"Holy shit, Hulk! Who knew you were more than just green muscles?" she grinned and shot up off the couch to approach me, a look of awe lighting up her face. "You aren't screwing with me, are you?"

"Not screwing with you."

"Fucking unbelievable. Better and better. My own personal, amazing, Incredible Hulk. Capable of busting down doors, taming Krakens, and making amazing video games. Just…wow. And I love it. This game. It's so, so good." Her words had come out slower, tapering off toward the end of her sentence the closer she got to me.

My heart kicked up its pace.

By then she'd stepped over Kraken and around the couch, keeping me in her sights, her determined momentum bringing her flush against me. Without pause, she ran her hands up my chest to twine her fingers in the hair at my nape.

Then she pulled my head down, and laid the hottest, sexiest kiss of my life on my lips.

The groan that rumbled up from my chest was instantaneous.

Sweet, soft, succulent lips were plastered to mine. A cloud of that fresh citrus that I associated with her surrounded me. She took sucking, nibbling bites of my lower lip that had me spiraling with molten heat pumping heavily through my veins.

"Fuck, you're hot, Blast," I breathed against her lips, taking a moment to finally pull the sticks loose from her bun. Her blond tresses tumbled down her back, and I wrapped my fingers through it.

"Shut up and kiss me, Hulk," she threatened, nipping my bottom lip gently, like she was ready to throw down.

Another rush of heat swamped my cock, and I couldn't stop the harsh, panting breath or the guttural moan that escaped.

"Fuck yeah."

I took this shit over. Pulling her head back with a tug of my fist, I sank back into the kiss, licking past the seam of her lips to own the inside of her mouth.

Kissing her was like being immersed in the best gaming world that you never wanted to leave. Tongues tangling and rubbing, sensation building bigger than I'd ever felt before, I was desperate to taste and feel all of her soft parts.

"It's not enough," Blessing hissed, her leg curling around my thigh.

"Let me help you."

I reached down to palm her ass with both hands, hoisting her up against me, wanting to feel the heat at the apex of her thighs on my cock, which was already leaking precum. Her long legs wrapped around my hips automatically, and the monster reared his thick head against her cleft in approval, heavy and pulsing with a need that had been denied over and over again.

"Yes, Hulk. Like that," she whispered against my lips between soft, wet kisses.

"You like the monster rubbing on your pussy, Blast?" I asked gruffly, helping her grind.

"More than you know."

"I think I do know. You taste so good, baby. Do you taste this good all over?"

"You'll have to find out."

Walking the smattering of steps toward the door without letting go of her lips, I shoved her up against it and took over. Rubbing slowly against the core of her fire with gentle strokes. We both groaned in time with the rhythm of the grind. It was too good. Too much. Too fast. Too soon.

She was going to make me come in my pants. I hadn't done that since I was a kid.

Breath mingling, growing faster, when a final burst of rational thought broke through the haze of need. She still didn't know who I was. I didn't want her to hate me for this. We had to do this right.

I stilled, grimaced.

"What?" she cried out breathlessly. "Why did you stop?"

Looking down at her swollen, dewy lips and dazed expression didn't let me focus. Instead, I was thinking what a good look that was on her. So I set her down gently.

"What is it?" she asked again, confused. Then a flash of disappointment. "Did you come?"

I laughed without humor, looking down at the monster between us. "Hardly. This is killing me, but I'm trying to be a good guy here."

"Really? You're saying that now?" she practically snarled at me with her "mad kitten" face, and it told me I was doing the right thing.

"Yes. I need to be a good guy now. We need to talk. There are some things you need to know about me." I had a feeling her nephews would come home soon. We needed a stretch of time that would be uninterrupted.

"Wait." She narrowed her eyes suspiciously. "You aren't married, are you?"

"God no," I shook my head. "No way. But I'll need some time to share some things with you. What about dinner? Tonight?" And because I couldn't help myself, I caged her against the wall again with my hands on either side of her head. Leaning down, I placed a gentle kiss on her lips, this time nibbling on her sweet bottom lip.

"I have my nephews," she warned on a sigh, nibbling back, getting back into the groove of things.

"Maybe I can bring some take out." I pulled away from her delectable lips to lick and suck at her soft neck. She shivered delicately with another mewling sound of pleasure. Taking a deep breath, I finally pulled back, knowing we needed to separate if I was going to do this right. "We can talk after dinner. Do the guys have homework to do?"

"They need to study, so yeah. I can scoot them off to work in the office downstairs."

"What would you guys like to eat?"

"Well, we had pizza last night."

"All right. No pizza. What about Thai?"

"Perfect."

"Any requests?"

"As long as you include some yellow curry and vegetables with some rice, you can bring anything else. The boys eat a lot. They finished off a large pizza between the two of them last night. Hope you've got your wallet."

I grinned, something I'd been doing a lot since being around her. "Seven okay, Blast?"

"It is, my Hulk."

Could I give up the job for the girl? I'd never really thought about letting this ball drop. I'd been juggling so many for so long. There was nothing stopping me at this point. Something to think about. Hard. Fast. Now. Because if I wasn't part of the company, I would never want her to sign a contract with them.

I hoped she still thought of me as her Hulk after tonight.

Chapter 8
Blessing

We almost fucked.

Holy shit, we almost fucked against the door. But this was so fast! How was this happening so fast? It was like dynamite went off every time we were within touching distance. We were explosive. It was like, our thing. That, and grinding on each other.

My pussy was still throbbing and wet. I was still shaky with the arousal coursing through my veins. It was scary how good this was between us.

But he lived next door. This was bad on so many levels. I couldn't seem to do relationships. First there was the fact that I was weird. It had been a painful lesson to learn as a kid, one that taught me that violence was oftentimes absolutely necessary. So were demonic threats and painful sucker punches to the guts and gonads. Particularly when you were smaller and smarter than everyone else. I used the element of surprise to my advantage.

Over time, kids stayed away from me in general.

Except for Spiderman, who I basically bullied into being my friend. Outside of him, I was forced to learn the value of "me" time. I'd spent a lot of time alone. Trained myself to it over years. There were needs that still required action but being horny was something I usually handled myself. I had toys in both nightstands.

That had been challenging. My sex drive was healthy, and I wasn't ashamed of it.

There'd been a few guys over time who'd been enjoyable, but it'd never worked out for long. I was opinionated. Over the top. Too much to handle. Bossy.

Those were some of the problems guys had had with me when we parted ways.

Most had first been attracted to my cosplay before ultimately rejecting it. They didn't get it. They didn't understand why I wore it. And no one had felt the need to ask why it was something I enjoyed doing. There had yet to be anyone who wanted to understand me. Know me. Get me on a deeper level.

There'd been one guy I'd actually liked, a finance guy who was smart and fun, but the novelty of me had worn off. After a few weeks of fucking and playing games, he'd ghosted on me. It had hurt some. I'd had relationship goals. Dreams of a future where maybe there could be kids.

But that was probably the time I realized that not everyone got married. Not everyone was made for a partnership. I had definitely never met anyone who was a good counter to my less than typical personality and lifestyle.

Not gonna lie, though: My Hulk had some hot moves. I loved being manhandled. And he had the Hulk muscles to do it. He just picked me up, shoved me against the wall. I *wanted* him to throw me around a little. Toss me on the bed. Play with me like I was his fuck toy. Shit. I was getting myself worked up all over.

And he was going to come over soon. What was I going to do? Jump him again? Climb him like a tree? Yank his pants down his long thick legs to get some one-on-one time with his cock? Fuck that was a bad idea. But I couldn't seem to help myself. I turned into this siren whenever he was around.

That was a costume I needed. The Siren.

In any case, I was definitely going to show him my work.

I mean, it was only fair, right? I'd seen his game-soul, and now it was time to show him mine.

But it was turning me into a basket case. Why? I wasn't sure.

What the hell was wrong with me?

Added to that, I'd decided to work on my game—my baby—to kill some time and be productive until dinner when Hulk, was going to show up, so my nerves were strung out in no time flat. I was walking a thin line of looking like I had my shit together when I was one bad turn away from maniacal, cackling laughter. Not really…Maybe?

Of course, the ever-present glitch was like having a hot poker stuck perpetually in my eye. I was sure the left one was twitching. Rhythmically. Dammit. So I started looking at finishing my work on my huge, epic forest maze, but a big question kept popping up like an annoying gnat:

Would he like it?

What if he didn't like it? What then?

That was when I had to eyeroll myself, giving a snort at my own ridiculousness. *What if he didn't like it?* Well, I'd stab him in the neck with his own fingers, of course. Headbutt him across the bridge of his nose and watch his blood spurt. I snorted again at the image; I had to acknowledge why some guys couldn't "handle" me or my sense of humor.

Okay, no, really. What would I do if he didn't like it?

Nothing. That's what I would do. Since when did I let a man dictate how I felt about my work? If he didn't like it, he didn't like it. End of story. And, he could take a long hike off a short pier. Jump out of a plane without a parachute.

Yeah. That was how my thinking continued for the next few hours. Half excited with anticipation. Half ready to vomit because only Pedro and his team had seen this work before, but Pedro didn't count because he was like the brother I never had. A brother from another mother. Spiderman and Batman, saving the world together.

"Hey Blessing!" the boys shouted jointly from down the hall.

I followed their voices, finding them in the kitchen still dripping salt and sand on the tiles while they stood with the fridge door open, just staring into it. Disappointment, the kind of despairing expressions that only teens could emote with such acute feeling, morphed across their faces. I couldn't blame them. I often looked into my fridge wearing that face, and I was the one who did my own shopping.

"You look so sad. I can't stand it. We're having Thai takeout," I interjected, "so don't worry about the state of my fridge."

"Yeah? When?" Finn asked, excitement lighting up his features. Any promise of good, greasy, salty food brought light shining to their young, innocent eyes. "I'm so hungry."

I looked at the clock. "Maybe half an hour?"

The crestfallen look was back on his face.

"We'll go shopping for more food tomorrow. I

promise."

"You said that yesterday," Cody scowled.

"Well, this time I mean it." I smirked. "Hey, you could clean up the mess you're leaving on my floor. Leave your boards out on the patio, use your towels to wipe up the floor, and go get cleaned up. That should take up half an hour easily. Then you can play games until it's here."

"If I haven't passed out from hunger yet," Finn huffed a sigh.

"If my stomach hasn't eaten itself," Cody grumped.

"Gosh, I really hope neither of those things happen. Of course, it would be kind of interesting to actually see a stomach eat itself. Does it have a mouth? Will it burp when it's done? What if it gets sick? How will it empty itself out?"

"Blessing, you are totally twisted," Cody grinned, clearly going along for the temporary ride. It was a win.

"Look. I'm not a mom. I don't have a mom purse with everything but the kitchen sink, and I don't have a cupboard full of snacks. I will do my best to take care of you guys for four more days. But you have to know that it can't be too easy or comfortable for you because then you'll want to move in, and it'll really cramp my style."

"Whatever," Finn laughed. "I know you love us."

"More than I love myself." I grinned back. "Get cleaned up for food. I think it will probably be here soon."

"Wait. You don't know for sure?" Finn asked, a bit suspiciously.

"No. I mean, I know, sort of, approximately when it's coming." That damn flush was happening again. My face heating up. "So, uh, my neighbor from next door is coming with the food."

"The big-ass dude who kicked in the door yesterday?" Cody asked.

My heart pounded a little harder thinking of all that had transpired since that moment. I tried to keep my voice neutral. "That's the one."

Cody watched me a beat, the beginning of a knowing grin quirking his lips. "Is something going on with this guy?"

"What?" I tried to show surprise, but my expression felt overly exaggerated, like a caricature of what the expression was supposed to look like. Still, I went for it. Owned it. Tried to play this moment off like I hadn't already felt Ian's dick, the monster, pressing up against me, or that I nearly consumed him, feasting on his delicious lips earlier. "No way. That's silly. He's my neighbor. That would be uncool. Rule number one in life. Right? Remember that."

"I don't understand this whole rule thing." Finn decided to get in on the conversation with a cheeky grin. "But, I think you like him. I think you want him to be your boyfriend."

"Blessing has a boyfriend?" Cody bantered back with a look of mock surprise at his brother, engaging in some improv. "Since when?"

"Since the dude next door showed off his manly muscles," Finn played along, being the butthole that only a teen could be.

I rolled my eyes, needing this to end. "You know what I really like, my lovely nephews? A kitchen floor that doesn't have salt and sand on it. Go take care of that. Now. No food for you until it's done. I promise you that. Zilch. Empty bellies that eat themselves."

"Okay, okay," Finn held up his hands in surrender. "We're just playing around. Mostly. Except, I still think you like this guy."

"You know she does," Cody murmured, the devil in his blue eyes.

All I had to do was give them my stink eye, and they backed off.

They were good guys. There might have been a few grumbles, but they went off to do exactly what I said with Kraken shadowing them to sniff everything that had come in from the beach. I had to admit, the big beast was starting to look right, moving comfortably through the apartment. He'd managed to make an impression on me in a single day.

Was I becoming an easy mark? First, I'm thinking about adopting a homeless man's Rottweiler; then, I'm thinking about getting naked with my neighbor because licking the muscles of his abs seems like a very worthy, necessary task all of a sudden. And I was going to show him what was most important to me.

Maybe it was time to reevaluate my life? Another time.

Catching a glimpse of myself in the mirror, I saw that it was time to freshen up and get ready for the second half of my evening. While being in cosplay was fun and inspired me, I was not opposed to getting comfortable.

After taking a quick shower, I grinned at the chopsticks I used to twist my hair up into a bun, wondering if Hulk was going to pull them free again some time tonight. Sliding simple yoga pants up my legs, I added a hoodie and left my room to find the boys were already lounging on the couch playing Ian's video game.

Ian's game, *Terminus*.

It sounded so official.

Would my game sound official?

Blessing's game, *Multiverse Infinity*. My computer room called to me, so I went.

I lingered there, in my work room, studying the first drawing I'd completed as a child. It was framed behind glass, a prototype drawing of what ultimately came to be Sage, the character that recognizes all players' completed tasks, acts of heroism, and provides rewards for them with different levels of game currency.

On the old paper, she had wild black hair and deep blue eyes, while the rest of her remained a pencil sketch with some warrior clothing I thought was cool at the time. I hadn't been entirely sure of what her wardrobe would be when I was that age.

She'd been refined over time. Was now more three-dimensional.

It made me realize how close we were to completing the first edition of *Multiverse*. Just needed polishing touches here and there. A few weeks, maybe? If we could fix the damn glitch.

Goosebumps popped up on my forearms. I loved the sound of it. It made me sound legit. It made me feel like a badass. When the glitches were all worked out, and it was a freestanding piece of interactive artwork that the world would have access to, it would be ridiculously amazing. There weren't words to express the enormity of finding the end of the yellow brick road that first began in my make-believe world when I played alone in the backyard or on the playground as a child.

There was a knock on the sliding glass patio door.

My heart skittered a few beats up in my throat. I heard the boys answer, followed by some kind of pleasant greetings between the three of them. I couldn't make out the exact words, but it likely had something to do with the fact that the boys were playing the hell out of his game, too. They were clearly eager to ask him some questions, but he left them there.

Then came the sound of his echoing footsteps, in the hallway on the hardwood flooring. I'd told the boys to send Ian this direction when he arrived.

I felt him before I saw him. Goosebumps. Tingles. My body gave up a shiver that ran the length of my spine and hardened my nipples instantly. He was here.

This was my private room. The inner sanctum. If anyone could understand this place, it would be a fellow designer, someone who truly understood the beauty of the virtual world we lived in. Someone who might understand how this room represented the heart of me.

His steps halted just inside the room. The silence remained. It was thick. Building the longer I stood with my back to him. I lingered in my spot because, if I were being honest, I was afraid of what I might see on his face.

What would be bad?

A smirk? A grin? The absolute worst would be if he had a blank face, like he had to school his expression to keep from hurting my feelings or something like that. *Ugh. Just stop. Face him already.*

Gathering myself, I turned away from that first drawing on the wall, the genesis of Sage, and saw him there. Larger than life. My own personal Hulk, taking up most of the doorway with his body. Broad. Muscular. Worn jeans hung from his lean hips. A long-sleeved, army-green Henley with a stylized neckline that had a couple of buttons near the hollow of his neck outlined his sexy, muscular build. And his hair was still damp, finger combed, so it was unruly.

Fuck, he was a specimen. And I liked him. Like, I really, really liked him. How did that happen in just a day or two? My breath hitched involuntarily at the realization. Was he actually my kind of people? My heart squeezed with the thought. Shit! What was I doing? Setting myself for even bigger heartache?

It was too much to think about now.

Instead, I studied the masculine angles of his face, zeroed in on his reaction to my work. Studied it sharply…and felt a taste of relief and pleasure. There was a look of awe.

"Blessing…" he rumbled in his low voice, his bright eyes scanning the room looking like his mind was blown.

I turned my own gaze on the room to try and see it through his fresh eyes.

Steampunk meets modern tech with my desk,

which had large, black metal gears for table legs and a desk lamp that was also a microscope. But sitting on top of that L-shaped slab of rough-wood desk sat three sleek computer monitors attached to my system and keyboard.

The other side of the room had bookshelves pushed up against the wall that were made entirely of rusted metal piping. They housed all of my old textbooks, industry books, comics I'd devoured as a child, and showcased a variety of old video game cases. In front of that was my drafting table, much in the same furniture style as my computer desk but holding all of my art supplies.

However, none of this, nor any of the various steampunk-ish paraphernalia scattered around the room, caught his attention.

Instead, he was mesmerized by what was beyond all that.

Drawings in all shapes, sizes, and colors took up every available inch of wall space. This was what I'd been most nervous about him seeing. The growth and development of my project. Its evolution from infancy to its final incarnation.

He moved closer to the wall, inspected one of the studies, drawings done in series within a story panel from my game. It demonstrated the progression of a game aspect, from being an overly large, simple sunflower to becoming a personalized, handheld helicopter. He moved on to another drawing where a spikey pod from a tree could turn into a swinging mace for protection. Would he appreciate the steampunk aspect of it all? It was a form of my own spiritual alchemy. One thing becoming something else. Nothing could be underestimated in this game. The most innocuous thing could be an escape, a clue, or a weapon.

"If you couldn't tell, I'm creating a game. It's almost done, actually. It's called *Multiverse Infinity.*"

I found myself standing next to him, not sure when my feet had spontaneously moved me across the space. Near enough that I could lean into him, I tried to see what he was being drawn to, follow his progression of study around the room as his eyes traced all of the lines I'd painstakingly drawn over the years.

My nerves got the best of me when he remained silent. I found myself narrating the moment.

"There are ten different worlds to navigate, so ten planes that are each their own world with their own set of rules, accessed through hidden portals that require game quests to be found. But there are also secret portals that open worlds within worlds on each level. They become necessary not only to a quest on the plane where they exist but also to future quests on other planes. I have plans to add more in a second edition, but I'm getting ahead of myself. I need to get this one done first."

He was still moving around the perimeter of the room. Still not talking. Just this intense study of each of the images. I took a deep breath. Started feeling overly warm. Cleared my throat. Tried to fill the void.

"I spent a lot of time on my own, growing up. Had a lot of time to think. Too much, maybe." I gave a shake of my head as we moved on down the wall of drawings. "I figured it would be interesting to turn things that were innocuous into powerful items. A beautiful sunflower that becomes an escape mechanism. A leaf that becomes a shield. I wanted everything to have the ability to become more than what it looked like. To be able to..." I floundered for a word. My brain seemed to have gone on a hiatus.

"Transform?" he finally spoke, asking the word as a question. He stopped, his eyes capturing mine. Holding me there without lifting a finger, but it was in that moment I could see the reverence that was reflected in their depths.

He got it. I knew he'd get it.

"Transform. That's exactly right." A gentle breath escaped from between my lips. I hadn't realized I'd been holding it.

There was a gravitational pull his direction. I found myself crowding closer toward him, looking up into the deep well of his eyes. His scent, a mix of some kind of spicy soap, clouded around me.

Damn he smelled good.

As though he couldn't help himself, his hands landed on my hips, slid down over my ass, and picked me up, lifting me so I was eye level with him. The power of his blue-green gaze, the way it seemed to see into and through me, pierced my soul. There had never been anyone who'd made me feel like this before.

"You're even more amazing than I could have known," he said in his rumbly, gruff tone that made my pussy instantly heat and swell. Was that his superpower? Could he, in fact, break doors with a single kick, tame beasts with a single command, and make me cream panties with a single look?

He put me on the stool at my drafting table, still standing between my legs, still keeping me mesmerized with a look.

He raised his hand, let his fingers hook strands of hair behind my ear.

More tingles returned. Centered in my lower abdomen. My yoga pants were about to need changing. They'd be toast before long. It was definitely hot in here. I could feel my cheeks starting to burn.

"Uh…so, what do you think of the work?" I whispered.

"It's a reflection of you." His vibrant eyes were locked on. Serious. A little awed. "You look around and see the greater, untapped potential, and you find a way to draw it out. For you, everything is always more than it appears. It's your take on the world. It's who you are."

My eyes burned with each of his words.

He was seeing me in a way that no one had ever seen me before. This time, the warmth created by his words was centered in my chest. There was a tender pinching sensation around my heart that I'd never felt before. It felt like, for the first time ever, a man I was interested in really was "my kind."

Could I accept that? Be open to it?

The sense of vulnerability had me breaking eye contact instantly to look at the wall again, and I was relieved that the moment was gone.

I needed time to think. To process. This was so much more than just fucking around with each other.

"Who are the main characters here?" he asked quietly, his hands caressing paths over the length of my thighs.

It was hard to think when he did that.

"Well, so, Sage is the gamekeeper, the main female deity. She awards quests and good deeds with the powers of transformation. Players are rewarded when building up, protecting, helping, engaging in teamwork, while, on the other end of things, killing unnecessarily and stealing have consequences. Powers are stripped. Special bonuses lose their magic. But the player doesn't know that right away. The yang to Sage's yin is Storm." I did a Vanna White sweep of my arm toward the other side of the room.

The drawing of Storm rested opposite her. Blonde, like me. His hair was short and spikey in places.

"Does he work to destroy?"

"That's his job. He sends out his minions to release biological warfare and wreak other kinds of havoc, which allows players to determine how they're going to handle their shit. The game ends with finding him and killing him, but that won't happen until the end of the second edition."

"A continuous morality play?"

"Yeah. That's about right."

"The drawings are so rich. The detail is mind-blowing. I don't have that kind of detail in my game. It's the piece that was missing for me."

"Art was my initial field of study. I majored in art and minored in computers. Learned how to bring art to the digital platform. Then, I kept taking different university extension classes to get more proficient with putting together code. I do have a good friend. Someone I grew up with, who helps me with the trickier aspects of putting it all together. His name's Pedro."

His eyes dropped for a moment, and when he looked back up, they had a hard edge.

"What's wrong?"

"Nothing." He shook his head, gave another scan of the room, this time it was just a quick flick of his eyes.

"Ian?" I frowned, but my question was interrupted by the sound of the doorbell.

His lips tight, he quirked a half smile my way. "Let's eat, but then there's something I need to talk with you about."

"You are sounding quite mysterious," I quirked a brow. "Should I be worried? Are you sure you're not going to tell me you have a wife and kids somewhere, and that I shouldn't have kissed you or something?"

He huffed a laugh and wrapped his big arms around me, pulling me close to his chest. It felt so good to be wrapped up in him, smelling him, feeling him. Could he be "the one"? I mean, whatever that meant, right? Not like I was a hearts and flowers kind of gal. I was a badass game designer who'd made bullies cry. But this was so nice.

No way... It was definitely too soon. That didn't mean we couldn't have some fun, right? I mean, it wasn't like there was a hallway monitor in our building. It was just the two of us. He had the south side, I had the north side, and we shared the dividing wall in-between, minus the small, square foyer outside of our front doors that housed the elevator and stairs up through the center of all three floors.

With his chin resting on top of my head, he murmured, "No hidden family. Definitely not that. Kissing you was lifechanging. I just want to put that out there while the boys are in the other room."

"Lifechanging, huh?" His words brought more butterflies to my heart area. If I wasn't careful, I was going to fall for him. Hard. It wasn't that other guys hadn't said sexy shit to me in the past when we'd hooked up, but it just hadn't mattered so much before. They hadn't mattered. Somehow, Hulk was shoving his way into my inner mental circle in a record period of time. No one had ever managed to get there. No one.

"The boys are starving," I sighed, my breath sounding a tad shaky.

"They told me they'd been surfing all afternoon. They offered to take me tomorrow when they're done with school. I figure I could maybe learn a new hobby since I'm at the beach. Offered to pay them for lessons."

"They'll be happy to get some extra dough. Then they can buy food because their auntie never has any." I smirked. "In any case, you'll have fun. But you'll need a wetsuit. It'll feel like freaking sub-zero out there right now."

"Blessing!" Finn shouted down the hall. "Food's here!"

I winced at the decibel. "Let's get them going."

Cody was already at the door taking bags when we walked down the hallway. The delivery guy gave a quick wave to us and headed off as he closed the door. Finn was changing the input on the television from gaming back to satellite.

The sudden change in background noise was startling. It went from a paused silence to some loud entertainment news. Tabloid gossip. Finn was looking for the secondary TV remote for the satellite to shut it off. It was somewhere in the cushions they'd displaced in seeking comfort.

"It smells so good," Cody groaned, unknotting the plastic bags the food was in.

Turning back from the cupboard with a short stack of paper plates, I saw Ian hovering near the table, just watching me. That one look lingered in his eyes. The one that said he'd just seen something new and amazing that he hadn't even known existed.

"Why make dishes, right?" My heart beat a little faster, my palms sweating as I approached him with the disposable plates. "Who needs extra work on a night like this?"

He was so hot. He was my Hulk. Standing there giving me that look. So fucking sexy. Maybe I'd have to overlook my rules. Fuck the rules, right? Rules were broken all the time. Rules were for people who weren't risk-takers. Who were uptight with sticks up their asses. I did not have a stick up my ass, and I was not uptight. The verdict was in. It was being decided in my favor.

Jump him. Get naked with him. Let us see where this went. Definitely.

"Uh…Ian? Is that you?"

"What?" Ian turned to where Finn was staring at the TV.

Spinning back to look at the TV, I frowned my confusion. It was definitely him. His rugged face filled up the screen of my large-screened TV. My eyes rounded, taking it all in.

It was a still shot at some past dinner event where he was standing at a podium giving a talk. The captions "Gamecon" and "New CEO or No Go?" were splashed under it. The host of the show, some young guy with pants that were too tight and hair that was overly processed, wore a big grin as he reported excitedly.

"…the rumor I'm hearing is that Ian Patrick is out and Josh Henderson is in! Known as 'The Shark' to those in his professional circle, Ian is known for attracting big talent with many of the gaming world's finest RPG designers. He's hosted panels at Comic Con for the last five years, bringing attention and big money to a company that was in decline before he joined the team. According to business insiders, he's more than doubled Gamecon's net worth in the short time he's been there. While he seemed like the obvious choice for

navigating the company successfully into the future, a little bird in the company has spilled that Harvey Stevens wants to go a different direction. We'll see if the president of Gamecon is onto something. Who knows? We'll have to wait and see what happens."

My heart was pounding hard, but this time, for an entirely different reason.

Throat suddenly dry, likely because my jaw had dropped open as I listened to the report, I tried to process what I'd just heard. As though in a dream, I turned to look at him. There was remorse there. A sadness to his eyes.

He was sad? You've got to be kidding me.

I was the fool. So stupid. I was the one thinking hearts and flowers like a dumb girl. I'd been the one who'd been throwing myself at him. Kissing him. Showing him the secret places in my soul. Meanwhile, he'd been working me. I was such an idiot.

"I was planning to talk to you after dinner," he said quietly.

"Get. Out." My face heat-flashed red as a mixture of shame and betrayal crashed down all around me. It had all been a façade. A house of cards. No wonder it fell.

He took a breath, held out his hands as though he was trying to calm a wild animal. "It's not what you think. I'd really like the chance to explain."

"You mean, you don't want my game?"

"No, I do. Your game is the best thing I've seen in years."

"Then what is there to explain? How you played me?" My voice cracked. I took a moment to look away. Clear my throat. Shake my head at my own foolishness.

"It wasn't like that," he scowled, anger sharpening his words. "It's never been like that with you." But he didn't say anything further.

"So moving in next door was a coincidence?" The layers of this started settling in, and I gasped a breath. My anger was turning volatile the longer I stood there. "You moved in next door! What the actual hell is that about?"

"If we're going to talk, let's do it outside," he growled quietly.

That's when I noticed the twins standing frozen, unsure of what to do—eat or get protective on my behalf. I took a couple of breaths. Inhaled, exhaled. Then faced the boys.

"It's all fine, guys. Have some food. I'm going to talk to Ian out in the hall." I stomped my way toward the door, throwing a deadly look at him over my shoulder.

Furious was an understatement.

"Are you sure?" Finn asked, clearly wanting to "stand up" and do the right "man" thing.

"I'm sure. I just need to give this guy a piece of my mind, and you know, I wouldn't want you losing your good opinion of me if you hear the words I'm going to use." I tried to toss a reassuring grin their way, but I was fairly certain it probably looked like a teeth-baring grimace instead.

The moment the door closed with us out in the hallway, Ian looked down at me moodily. "I saw your work at Pedro's house a few months back. It was fucking riveting."

"Spiderman? Oh my god," I closed my eyes and shook my head. "You're Pedro's friend. The 'genius.'" I air quoted at him.

"I am, and you need to know that he had no idea I was moving in next door."

"Yeah, the creeper move, right? I guess I should be flattered that you went through a lot of trouble for me, but with companies like yours, it's anything for the big bucks, right? It all gets written off anyway."

"This is the only time I've done this. The integrity of your design, the beauty in the art, the genius of your concept was something that grabbed me instantly. I knew instantly that I needed to be part of your project in some way."

There was sincerity in his gaze, but I didn't want to acknowledge it. My heart was actually paining me. What the fuck?

"I get it. So you worked me. Fucking pro. No wonder you're 'The Shark.' You got invited into my house. You got into a room that no other person has ever been invited into." I thought about that, and I got an actual chest pain. "Here I was thinking you were someone I could really be with. What a laugh. I just dove right into that one. Such a fucking idiot."

"You're not an idiot," he growled his own frustration, "and I wasn't playing you. Just the opposite. The meeting was so important to me that I wanted to make it right. But then that whole thing happened with Kraken, so I decided I was going to tell you tonight."

"Why not sooner?"

"When we were running around in our underwear? Tell me how that conversation should have gone? Seriously. I just kicked in your door, I'm wearing boxers, and my dick is happy to see you. Is that when I'm supposed to say that I'm the guy who thinks you're incredible, that your work is amazing, that I haven't been able to think straight because it was so amazing that it inspired me to start looking at my own design work again?"

"Fuck, I'm a moron," I shook my head, not wanting to hear him. I looked down at my shoes to hide the pathetic, glassy tears in my eyes. "I made it easy."

"You aren't hearing me, Blessing."

"No, I'm not, Ian." I made a point of using his name rather than my nickname for him, blinking like mad to clear away the tears that wanted to spill.

I did a quick swipe under my eyes to get rid of the offensive moisture. "My time for listening to you was at any point before that news show."

"Fuck," he ran his fingers through his hair before he pierced me with those beautiful eyes again. "Blessing. It was like, once I saw you, I had to know you. You were brilliant and beautiful and bigger than life, and Pedro couldn't say enough about you. I had to be around you. I needed to understand what it was about you that made me wish I were doing something else, that made me not only forget my own personal rules, but not give a shit about following them anymore. It was like you bewitched me."

"Bewitched, huh?" I sneered, squinting up at him.

He pushed off from the wall to crowd me against the wall next to my door, caging me in with his arms. "From the moment I saw you, I stopped being able to recognize my actions. I was making impulsive decisions, like buying this place next to you. I couldn't stay away. You're like this sorceress, casting spells. That's how suddenly my life changed because of you."

I let myself enjoy the feeling of his big, masculine energy for just a moment. I figured I owed myself that since I was giving up something that I didn't think I'd ever feel. I gave him a grin, but he could tell it contained no warmth. His own eyes narrowed, studying me.

"Bewitched, huh?"

"Yes. I'm caught up in you. Happily. For the first time in a long time."

"Oh, I'll cast a spell on you," I murmured, wanting to leave him as horny as I felt every time he was around because fuck him. Fuck him, fuck him, *fuck* him. He turned out to be a fucking lying liar when I was thinking he might be my perfect match.

I grabbed his head and pulled him down for a hard kiss that instantly had his arms wrapped around me, pulling me close. I gloried in the taste of him, licking past the seam of his lips and rubbing against his tongue, empowered by the sound of his groan. Appreciating the feel of my pussy getting hot and swollen.

I slid my hands down his abs, letting my nails scrap down his six pack over his shirt. Muscles jumped, flexed, tightened under my touch. My fingers ran a path down his muscular thighs, outlined by his worn denim, until my fingers found their target. His cock was hard. I wrapped my fingers around it with both hands. He broke our kiss, hissing on a breath of air when I gave it a squeeze and rubbed it, pulling at it.

"Fuck," he muttered against my lips before closing his eyes, his forehead resting on mine, his eyes closing with the pleasure of my touch.

"You like when I touch you?" I taunted.

"I need you to touch me," he growled, his teeth clenched.

My fingers kept rubbing on him, encouraging him to grow bigger.

"Is that right."

"Yes." His voice was a tortured sound against my lips.

"Then listen up. Each and every time you see me, hear my voice, or so much as think about me," I breathed intimately right back, "you will remember this moment when I had your cock in my hands, and you will instantly get hard. Every single time. And you will know that there is nothing you can do about it because I want nothing to do with you."

I ducked out from between his arms, hand on the doorknob. Forced a cold expression on my face.

"Fuck. That's too bad, Blast," he huffed in a low, angry voice, as he pushed off the wall to stand at his full height. Looking down at me, he added, "because I came here for you. But I can be patient. This is bigger than right now. I'm only just figuring some things out in my life. But I'm going to wait until you're ready to hear it. And I'm sorry you found out this way instead of the way I'd planned. Maybe when you cool off, you'll let me apologize and explain." He shoved through his own door a half a dozen feet away on the other side of the elevator and slammed it shut.

I'd wanted to be the one to walk away, but he'd beat me to it. And now I was left with a feeling of being unfair to him. Not letting him explain. Fucker. I didn't want an explanation. I wanted people to be upfront about who they were. From the start.

I went back into my own place to encounter two boys in the kitchen, still uncertain as to what they should do.

"Everything okay?" Cody asked. It was heartwarming to see that they hadn't touched the food he'd brought. They were trying to show loyalty in their own way. And they were hungry, too. My eyes burned again.

"It's all good. We had it out." I motioned to the cartons of food. "Eat up. Don't waste that. There are starving children in the world and all that."

"There are starving children in this kitchen," Finn muttered.

"Are you sure you're okay?" Cody was still rooted to his spot, his sweet face lined with concern, staring down at me. That was going to break me. His sweetness and unquestioning support.

"It's fine. I just misunderstood some things. Nothing I feel like talking about." I huffed a laugh. "Seriously, eat the damn food and study for your finals. The semester ends this week, right?"

"Yeah. We have a Calc final tomorrow."

"I hope you've got that under control because at

this point, I can't help you. I get confused counting on my fingers."

Finn laughed as expected, but Cody seemed to have suddenly grown an inch in maturity, because he was looking at me with a soft expression and just nodded. He was acknowledging my attempt to get past the moment with some humor.

"We're good with our math, Blessing."

"Awesome. Count your blessings, right?" I arched a brow.

It wasn't until a few hours later that I found myself sprawled on my bed, the moment anticlimactic. I'd begun the evening thinking that maybe we'd be starting something new here, only to end up back in the same place as before. No, it was worse, actually. I'd believed we were actually compatible. There hadn't been other guys I'd actually thought about the same way.

So I'd thrown myself at him. Fucking embarrassing.

A groan startled me from my thoughts. Looking around, I recognized I was alone in my bedroom, but somehow, it sounded like someone was right here. The groan sounded again. *What...?*

Quietly getting up from my bed, I tiptoed around to locate where I thought I heard the sound and discovered a vent.

Holy shit.

Ian and I shared the wall in our bedrooms.

"Fuck..." I heard him growl, his breathing growing louder, heavier. He groaned again, and I realized I was hearing him stroke himself off. *"Fuck me...Blessing...Blast..."*

Was that my...

Did he just say...

Oh, fuck. The image of him tugging one out with my name on his lips not only let me know he was into me, but also caused sudden heat to engulf my sensitive girl bits, and I almost groaned with the feel of it. Silently, I slid to the floor, briefly questioning and discarding the idea that I'd give him privacy for this. No fucking way.

This belonged to me.

His orgasm was mine.

My curse had worked.

Chapter 9
Ian

Her fucking curse had me feeling blue balls all night, even after jerking off twice, once last night and once in the shower this morning.

Remembering her hand squeezing me, just like she said. And there it went again. It was awkward, getting an erection when I was talking with Sal on the phone. All I could do was adjust myself and shake my head.

"Serious shit is going down in the office."

"What's going on?" I asked, barely listening, which was strange. It was like I was a different Ian, or this was a different universe, a universe where I was more interested in watching the waves from my third story window. Somehow, I was less interested in any of the shit happening in the office when the secrets deep in my mind had revealed themselves to me. They were explaining my abnormal actions to me. Finally.

The surfers were out there, bobbing on the waves. The pull to experience that sense of peace was strong. I'd set up some lounge furniture in that corner of the room because of the view. I wanted to be able to disengage my brain, even if it was just for a few minutes of time. Watch the waves roll in. Watch the small dots on the waves, the surfers, bob up and down on their boards, becoming part of the powerful swells that were somehow bigger than all of the bullshit in this world.

"Josh came by last night and again this morning," Sal murmured as quietly as he could from his desk space in the bay area office, not wanting to be heard. "Fucking prick. Said he was the new boss in town and demanded I show him what you were working on. I came back from the bathroom, and he was at my computer."

An involuntary huff of laughter barked from my chest. I wasn't surprised, but I had assumed Harvey was smarter than this. That was a good lesson to earn. Don't underestimate someone's stupidity. No one had called to inform me yet, but I'd already put some things in motion with HR. My actions created a low-level anxiety, but I was riding that out.

Besides, I was still beat from a restless night.

"Don't worry about it."

Surprisingly, I wasn't even upset. I had other

options and a shit ton of money I'd invested. My mom was right. I had more money than I could ever spend in a lifetime. Embracing this new change left me with options if I let it. My mind needed to release the stranglehold on this job, this need I had to control this one thing, my work. Once that happened, once I really let my psyche do that, the fear and anxiety might also, finally, dissipate.

I hadn't realized how scared I'd been of losing my mom, especially after the few close calls we'd had during the ups and downs of treatment. In a world where I couldn't control whether she lived or died, it made sense that I'd grab hold of whatever I could. And in this case, it was my job and the sense of false security it created.

But it did leave me in an interesting place. Used to being in perpetual motion, I wasn't sure what I was going to do now. There was no way I planned to retire from the industry.

For sure, I was leaving the company, but what I was going to do next, I didn't know. Take VisiStation up on their offer? It was a good one, very lucrative, but it wasn't sitting right with me. Didn't feel right. Being successful had been my sole purpose for so long...now what?

A random thought crossed my mind.

I needed to go see my mom. I wondered how she was doing. Was she eating well? Was she getting to her doctors' appointments? They needed to see her regularly. Make sure that shit wasn't growing inside of her again. But she was alive now, and I wanted to honor the time I still had with her.

A brief flicker of remembered fear made me wince. My heart clenched. I breathed through it. My anxiety wasn't a new experience. I'd been going through this same exercise, breathing through the ever-present fear, since she'd first told me of her diagnosis. Maybe it was my turn to heal.

My phone pinged with another incoming call. It was Josh. I ignored it, knowing it would piss him off. What he didn't realize was that I held all the strings to the clients with the big money. All of the contracts I'd worked on had an opt-out clause. They could walk at any time. I'd also made sure to contact all of them and let them know what was up and that they had options.

I chuckled to myself, but Sal heard it through the phone line.

"Dude, I don't think you understand. He wants to take all of your clients and make it look like he's a big hero, and Harvey sent me an email telling me to let him. He's also hunting the project that has you in Hermosa Beach. Wants all of the contact info on what you're working on, so he can hold the meeting himself."

I laughed out loud this time. "He doesn't even know what it's about. What an idiot."

"I told him I don't have it. That nothing official

has happened."

"I appreciate the update. Just keep holding down the fort."

"I'll be in touch later."

"All right, man. Thanks for the update."

Last night had been both beautifully surreal and harshly disturbing at the same time. So much so that I hadn't been able to fall asleep until it was almost light out. That meant I hadn't woken until past noon. I kept thinking about worlds, plural, that Blessing had created, the room where she did her work, how magical it had all seemed.

She'd made a brief appearance on the patio in the afternoon dressed as a god damn cheerleader, her little skirt barely covering her ass, her hair in two pigtails on either side of her head. The top had been cropped, and likely because it was cold, she didn't stay out long.

I'd gone to the door, hoping to have a minute to better explain myself, but she'd struck her pose, pressed both middle fingers to her lips where she licked each one, then flipped me off with both of them. So I left her alone. The display had been both disappointing and arousing at the same time.

My cock had risen for the show.

Clearly she was still mad, and I couldn't blame her. The hurt look on her face had been all my fault. She'd trusted me. Truthfully, there wasn't a way she would have welcomed me into her world if she'd known who I was. On some level, I knew that. It was likely the reason I'd dragged my feet in telling her. I knew it would change how she looked at me, and I wanted to be her personal Hulk. I wanted her to be my beautiful little Blast just a little longer.

It was so clear to me now. I'd come all this way for her, not just for the game. Even worse was knowing that when it came down to it, she wasn't wrong about Gamecon. There was no way I would ever want her to be part of that shitshow, not when I didn't have the controls in my hand.

Too little too late.

Still, I was so fucking sorry. Arrogance. That's what it came down to. I'd been hyper-focused for so long, learned the art of being cutthroat from the masters, only worried about making sure there was plenty of money… just in case.

I'd lost pieces of myself along the way.

Maybe I could get some of them back.

Being in Blessing's space had been yet another moment of Zen for me. It reminded me of how good I used to feel, how alive, when I worked my own designs.

She'd taken the time to create an inspiring workspace. Every piece of furniture was somehow leather or metal and looked like some kind of mash up of Mad Max meets Victorian England. I half expected everything within the room to be able to transform into something else. An abundance of drawings, creativity radiating out, leaving no wall space uncovered.

The raw art in its initial conception was everywhere I'd looked. It had left me speechless. She was actively living inside the world she created anytime she went to work on it.

There were drawings of lush plants that could have not only medicinal qualities but could also prevent further disease, based on the descriptions she'd written as captions. It was part of one of the quests if someone took the time to arm their healers in their villages with these plants.

We would get there together, not separately. That was the theme of this.

And being there with her, it just strengthened the connection. It was right. Here was exactly where I was supposed to be. Until the news came on. What the fuck happened there?

I spent the rest of the day unpacking a few of the final boxes that had arrived, arranging my office space downstairs and wondering if I was even going to be here long enough to figure out my next steps. Would it be better to head back to San Francisco? Give her back her space? Would that help to make amends?

When she was ready to hear it, I did need to apologize.

Sleep was hard to come by once again. I'd skipped my surf lessons, not wanting to put

Blessing's nephews in an awkward place. It was clear they were devoted to her. Not that I didn't still want to learn. It was just something I was going to have to figure out on my own. Others before me had done so.

I wondered if Blast had ever learned how to surf, which led me to thinking about how perfectly we fit together, how just being together made me want to go primitive on her ass.

Claim. Strip. Fuck. Own.

I'd had to rub another one out in bed. My fantasies were always revolved around what she wore. That cheerleader uniform had me envisioning her ponytails as handholds where she teased the big jock one too many times and had to pay up with a sexy blow job.

I'd come hard with that fantasy.

And now I was hard just remembering again. At least I wasn't on the phone anymore. I was playing my old video game on one of the few pieces of furniture that graced the sparse room. There were probably things I needed to do, but they no longer seemed that important.

"It's okay, Kraken," I suddenly heard her say through the vent. *"I'm okay. Aren't you a sweet boy. I was just being dumb. I thought he was going to be mine. Did you hear what I was calling him? It was stupid, right? I kept calling him my own personal Hulk. See? Dumb. But it's fine. Someone*

will be my Hulk one day."

That stung. It also made my blood hot, thinking of some faceless guy grabbing her ass. Pulling her close. Making her moan and shake.

And then she appeared on the patio again. I heard her sliding door and made sure to shove off the armchair for a better look. The best view was from my own glass door, and I took a position there to watch, needing to have her in my sights.

Then I got the full image.

Dressed in a Catholic schoolgirl's uniform, where the skirt was way too short, barely covering her ass, and her white stockings came up over her knee. Her hair was in a long braid and her white shirttails were tied up under her perky breasts that I wanted to do dirty things to.

Fuck me.

Just like she'd said, was it two nights ago? Whatever day. Time seemed irrelevant. She had me thinking about that last time we were out in the hall and her little hand was wrapped around my dick, pulling on it. She was a damned witch.

The monster was getting painfully hard. If she bent over the slightest bit, her ass would show, and I could see what color panties she was wearing today. Or was she wearing full-coverage, white cotton, schoolgirl panties? Imagining bending her over the lunch table she usually sat at was taking over my mind.

Should I go outside? Maybe she'd cooled off now. Maybe she'd hear me out today. But when I opened the slider, she struck a pose, lifted one of her middle fingers and kissed it, before going back inside her place. Nope. Not cooled off. At least we were down to one finger.

Somehow my life was imploding. The dominos were falling, and I didn't know how to stop them. Did I want to stop them?

It was time to do something different here.

I changed into my trunks, grabbed a thick hoodie and flipflops, and headed out toward the beach, figuring I could try to teach myself how to surf. It couldn't be that hard, could it? There was a surf shop on the pier. I could probably rent what I needed there.

It was two hours later, after getting tumbled through the waves, like a laundry load on the spin cycle that I realized how I'd had my ass handed to me by Mother Nature. Watching the other surfers had given the false sense of ease. They made it look effortless. As athletic as I was, I had to acknowledge that the waves were beating the shit out of me. Still, I kept at it.

By the time I'd finally managed to get up on my feet for a few seconds, it was a few hours later, the sun was getting low in the sky, and I was ready to collapse, but the sense of elation running through my bloodstream had a tired smile spreading across my face. I sat on the board on the beach and watched the waves roll in, finally able to enjoy the quiet of my mind.

Finding a true sense of peace took work.

"You did okay out there."

The twins appeared off to my left. They'd also been out on the waves, from the looks of it, and were peering down at me with closed-off expressions. It was hard to tell one from the other. There was a hint of aggression to their stance, like they needed to have it out with me.

There went my peace, but I totally understood.

"I appreciate that. How is Blessing today?" I asked, cutting to the chase.

"She's good," one of them said. "Mad, though."

"I know," I nodded. "She won't talk to me. I wanted a chance to ask for a formal meeting, but things went fucking haywire before I could do that."

"You really want her game?" the first kid asked.

"You've seen it, haven't you?" I asked.

"She doesn't show anyone," the other kid said, scowling down at me. "Were you just fucking with her like she said? Blessing is the coolest person I know, and if you were, I'd want to kick your ass."

I kept my eyeroll to myself, but I did stand up. They were tall, but I still had several inches on them and a whole lot more beef. They both stepped back, warily, recognizing they were getting in over their heads.

They needed to know that looking for a fight was the dumbest thing they could do.

"Seriously, guys, I know your heart is in the right place, but don't make fucking threats, ever, that you can't back up." I looked down into their eyes. They were wary now. "You could get yourself hurt. Secondly, I wasn't fucking around with Blessing. I wouldn't do that. I have only the utmost respect for your aunt, and I agree that she's fucking amazing. She's…special. I don't know what to do with that."

I turned back to the waves and watched as the sun touched the horizon, making the ocean ripple with a golden glow. There was a strange discomfort in my chest knowing that Blessing wanted nothing to do with me.

"You really do like her," the second kid said. They'd been studying my face.

"Pretty sure." Just thinking about her, that fucking schoolgirl uniform, was about to give me a chub, something I was actively fighting against in front of the guys. There were some things you just didn't do in public, and getting a woody was one of them.

Damn her. Witchy woman.

"Hey, we can still teach you to surf," the first kid was saying.

"You were doing okay, but we could give you some pointers for catching waves. If you're still interested in lessons," the second twin added.

I looked over at them wondering at their game. They were going to "beat" my ass a few moments ago.

"Blessing has never liked a guy before. Like, seriously liked. We don't want to see her get hurt, but we also think you're probably a good guy," the second guy tacked on.

"Thanks." I smirked.

"Tomorrow after school, we'll be here. And for the rest of this week," the first twin nodded. "We'll get you shredding instead of sucking water before we head home."

"All right."

It wouldn't hurt to have allies on the inside of her fortress. Maybe they'd put in a good word.

Chapter 10
Blessing

"So, he's a big-time game distributer who loves your game?"

Layla asked this question, eyes rounded innocently as she toyed with the straw in her iced tea.

Faker. I taught her that move. There was nothing innocent about what was happening here. I narrowed my eyes, sending death rays at her, knowing she was going to do to me what I would normally be doing to her.

Besides, I was already thinking that maybe, just maybe, I'd overreacted. I wasn't entirely onboard with that idea yet, but I could acknowledge that with the way we'd met, it would have been strange for him to come clean.

But, what the hell! He bought the place next

door.

Because he was so into me? Or the game? He said it was me, but see, he'd already acted like a big liar. Maybe not outright lies but lies of omission. Same effect. Was he ultimately going to feel like I was too much to handle, too opinionated, too loud, etc., etc., etc.? I mean, what did I really know about him?

Nothing. Except, well, he was willing to kick down my door to save me from an "attacker." Then he'd fixed that door without delay. He was not only into games, but he had created his own. He supposedly had a good work ethic and some integrity about his work. Pedro was friends with him, and that said something.

He could get my panties wet in nothing flat.

He was fun to be with.

I wanted to know more about him. Asshole!

The clash of different feelings was making me grouchy and snappish. I hated that.

"You're thinking so hard over there," Layla chirped innocently, a half-smile twisting one side of her mouth.

"Yeah, yeah," I grumbled.

I'd heard him jack off a couple of time with my name on his lips. Was it wrong that I went into my room to listen for it? I'd had a bead on the timing. Got lucky with it. It was fucking hot. He liked my Catholic school girl look.

In fact, I still had it on, which was weird because I was somehow more sensitized to the looks I was getting from rando guys. Note to self, remember to avoid overt flashes of skin when Hulk wasn't around to be tortured. Why it bothered me now, I didn't want to think about. I mean, it was just clothes, right?

Hmmm.

Now I wanted to know what he had me doing in his fantasies.

Not that I was going to do them.

See? This was all just the evidence I needed to nail the coffin shut on thoughts of a future relationship with someone. I was an oddball. How could I ever be taken seriously? *I* couldn't even get a handle on me. There also seemed to be a permanent chip on my shoulder because of the lackluster experiences I'd had with passionless guys in the past, and it was hard to keep failing at this one thing. Maybe I lacked that magic ingredient that others had.

"So, just to clarify. He loves your game, and he specifically came here to talk with you about it?"

"That's what he said. Who knows for sure," I muttered, sighing, letting my eyes drift to the overhead big screen TV that was playing a college football game. It had drawn a big crowd to the bar Zeke's on the Boardwalk, so the place was packed. Noisy.

A random evil thought came to mind. That's what I could do to further torment him. Wear a sexy football uniform. It was probably easy to find something online. For the last few days, I'd been dressing up in my sexiest costumes just to torment him.

If it were spring, I would have pulled out my coup de grace. My Princess Leia bikini from *Return of the Jedi*—the one Jabba the Hut had her in at the beginning of the film. That was every guy's fantasy, wasn't it?

That one had been waiting for me to find the perfect moment. This would have been it, if it weren't freaking cold outside, and if I hadn't had my teenage nephews around. No need to give them nightmares about their auntie.

But Layla wasn't done yet.

"And he moved in next door because he was so infatuated with you and your game? And he's hot. And you like him and want to jump him?"

"Yup." I let the "p" sound pop, then sighed, letting her savor this moment.

"I see what you mean. He's the biggest douche. You should sell this place. Move. Or, better yet, get a restraining order."

"That's not what I'm saying," I growled. I didn't even know what I was saying anymore. "He was using me to get close to my game. He was lying to me."

"For how long?"

"He was living there for a couple of weeks."

"But how long since you'd actually met him?"

"Two days."

"Yeah. That's what I thought. For two days, he was trying to figure out how to talk with you about a business opportunity, and probably only put it off because of the way you guys met. I mean, can we spell awkward? You knew the boxers vs. briefs facts about him before you even knew his name."

"Whatever." But I did know what his friend felt like, the "monster." He was a big friend. I'd thought about that friend of his, a bunch.

"I think you're putting him off because you're scared. There is finally a guy that you are interested in, who likes what you like, who is 'your kind', finally, but it's freaking you out."

"Why would that freak me out? I should be jumping for joy," I grumped, scowling at her. "That makes no sense at all. Really."

"You are so used to being in control of everything, that anything you can't control freaks you out. And you definitely won't be able to control him. But here's the funny thing; if you could control him, you would be back in the same boat you always find yourself in, and that is, pushing this guy away. The reality is that you do not want a guy you can control. Flat out."

"So, you're saying I'm a control freak?"

"That's exactly what I'm saying. You are this amazing force of nature, taking care of everyone around you, but no one is allowed to touch you. And that includes me, actually." There was a quick flash of realization in her deep blue gaze, like she just realized this. Her normally animated face muted. It was a slight shift of the facial muscles, but I could see it.

"That's crazy talk," I burst out, shaking my head to deny the idea. But she wasn't wrong. I had a sense of what she was trying to tell me, even as I said, "You're the best friend I have ever had."

"Which is the only reason I'm not all butt-hurt right now." She waved across the club to someone before turning back to me. "But partly, would we have become such good friends if I hadn't been a hundred miles of bad road? I mean, let's be honest. I was raw material, and that is right up your alley. What do I even bring to this friendship other than my absolute love and gratitude?"

There was a hint of vulnerability there in her eyes, and I realized that Layla didn't know how much she meant to me. How was it that I could think we were so close for the last two years, but she wondered how I felt. What was going on there? Was it me?

"Layla…" I wanted to talk about this, but she was waving it off, plastering a grin across her face.

"Really, it's no big deal."

But it was. How in the hell did I end up not only feeling like a fool for letting myself see hearts and flowers when I looked at Ian, but now my best friend had some kind of sense of alienation from me. What the hell?

"Hey Bet!" she grinned as Bethany, aka Malibu Barbie prototype, walked her sexy self over to our table looking nothing less than fabulous in her casual beachwear: a pale blue, filmy, off one shoulder top that tucked into her ultra-low rise, light wash jeans. She always looked like she was walking the runway.

"Layla," Bet acknowledged in her naturally husky voice, her doe-eyes taking in the scene critically. She had a way of analyzing and dismissing those she felt weren't a threat, which is exactly what happened when she gave me a side-eye before sitting with us.

"Aren't you working?" Layla asked, peering around Bethany and looking around the floor at the number of customers present.

"There's a big, tatted guy behind the bar who's trying to shoot fire at you through his eyeballs," I told her. The guy was impressive, able to send a smoldering glower her direction as he pulled a pint of something behind the bar. He looked scrumptiously pumped with the club's logo being stretched across his pecs, his biceps stretching the arms of the club's T-shirt.

Maybe he could be good for a night or two.
Maybe take the edge off. Help me forget about
Hulk. I mean, Ian. If Ian could see me come home
with this guy, I mean, that would make him burn.

"Oh him?" Bet waved her dismissive hand over
her shoulder in his direction. "That's Magnus.
Fucking workhorse. Doesn't believe in cutting
people a little slack."

"What kind of slack?" Layla frowned. "Don't
you get your breaks when you're here?"

"I get breaks, I take breaks, and I create breaks.
Then he gets mad because I'm flirting with the
customers."

"I'd take a break with him," I grinned, but Bet's
eyes snapped toward me in an instant. Her face
flushed as she looked me over again.

"He has a girlfriend." Her chin rose and her lips
tightened. Ah. She had a crush she didn't want to
admit to. Hmmm.

"Don't you dare lose this job." Layla put a hand
to her arm gently, but her voice was like steel. "I
went out on a limb for you with Mason, and I won't
appreciate you treating this opportunity like it's
trivial. Don't fuck around here or you and I will
have a permanent problem."

Bet's eyes suddenly watered, meeting Layla's
firm gaze, and I had to blink a couple times. That
was real emotion there. She was nodding her head
saying, "You're right. I'm being a brat, and you've

been a true friend. One I don't deserve."

"Hush. We all deserve support, and when we get it, we don't treat it like garbage," Layla lasered in with her newly found mom voice.

"You're right. I know. He just makes me so mad," Bethany ended on a hissing whisper, sweeping her golden blonde hair off her flushed face, and looking over her shoulder. He was still watching, handing back change to one of the customers.

"Order up, Bet!" Magnus called, a sharp note in his voice.

"Coming!"

"Yeah. So's Christmas," he responded impatiently.

Bet scowled a look his direction that could have not only set fire to the place but incinerated us all before standing up and marching to the bar, tray of drinks balanced on her shoulder. But while Layla was watching her with a small half-grin, I wanted to get back to the conversation we were having before Bet joined us.

"Layla," I reached across the table to take her hand. Her eyes found mine and I could see she knew I was serious. "You're right that I'm a bit of a control freak. When I was growing up, I didn't have a bunch of friends. There were mean kids who were not sensitive to someone like me who didn't fit a mold, so I learned to keep to myself. It trained me to be fierce because I could not show any weakness. That's who I was, for good or for bad. I had one good friend who needed me, and it's only been recent that I reached out to get his help on my work."

"The glitch?"

"Yeah. Pedro. Spiderman."

"It's all right. I mean, mostly, you've been lucky enough to have your shit together. What would you need from me anyway?" she said with a shrug, forced a smile on her face.

"No way." I shook my head, desperate for her to understand. "I rely on your kindness, your support, your acceptance of me and who I am. You know what it feels like. Kids used to make fun of me, and most normal people can't handle being around me, but you welcome all of my quirks. Fucking hell. You didn't blink an eye when I showed up dressed like Wonder Woman for Comic Con a few years ago. That's saying something."

"That's nothing," she flushed, but there was a brightness to her eyes.

It shamed me that I'd never expressed this to her before. There was definitely such thing as being too independent. I could see that. Where was the friendship if trust and vulnerability was only a one-way street? And that's what I'd been doing here. Letting her take all the risks and withholding all of my bullshit.

"You've shown me what it takes to be a true badass, confronting all that you've had to stand up to in the face of real terror, and it makes me proud to be your friend."

"You helped me," she protested.

"I might have helped you, but it was your ass on the line. And you rallied, over and over. I don't know if I could ever match you in courage. You are one of my heroes, L-pop." I bit my lip because it was on the verge of trembling. Emotion clogged my throat.

"Oh, shut up. You're going to make me cry," she muttered, but she squeezed my hand.

"So, yeah." She knew she could trust me, but I'd never had the chance to show her that I trusted her. It was time I did that. My heart pounded as I felt that moment of vulnerability, where I needed to be honest with myself. "I like this guy. From the moment we first made eye contact, it was like...like...instant..."

"Chemical reaction?" she offered.

"Yeah. Instant. Big. Powerful. At least for me. I felt like I knew him already. But for one thing, it's just too fast. Too much. Too powerful, you know? This can't be real. This isn't how it happens in real life with real people."

"Sure it does. You aren't a kid anymore. You've gone through your share of frogs. You know what you're looking for in a guy. There's nothing wrong with knowing that someone fits you. But that's not what's freaking you out."

"No."

"You're scared that you won't fit him."

"I've never fit in anywhere," I said, voice starting to tremble. "No one has grabbed me the way he has, and no one has understood me the way I think he might, but while I was sitting there thinking he was finally, maybe the perfect ying to my yang, he was trying to figure out how to pitch a contract to me."

Layla nodded, listening.

"While I was reveling in this amazing reaction that I'd never felt before, while I was so quick to open the doors to show him my soul when I'd never done that with any other person before ever, he was busy trying to figure out how to officially ask for my game rights."

Layla pushed her glass away and leaned onto the little table. "If that's all he was feeling, then I'm sorry, Blessing. But are you sure that's all he wanted? I thought he was into you. The way he looked at you the other morning was hot."

"He's a guy, and I'm not ugly to look at."

She snorted her humor. "Far from it."

"I kissed him." The words slipped out before I could stop them.

"You did?" She tried to fight the grin, but it stretched across her face.

"And it was so good. I was just so excited that I'd been playing his game, which was amazing."

"Wait, what?"

"I was playing a game he'd created, all night, before I knew it was his. It was from years ago when he was still in school apparently, but it had similar themes to mine." I'd played it last night, too. It was beautiful.

"So, he *is* your kind of person. It's like, fated."

"He's not. He gave into the gods of greed. He took the corporate job that gave him the big bucks. He made money more important than design." After seeing what he was capable of, that one act was pretty unforgivable. "He's Darth Vader."

"You don't know that. And besides, someone has to do that job, right?"

"Not the way his company does it. They are soul murderers. It's just the water he swims in."

"He might surprise you, B-girl. He literally moved his entire life to be right next door to you. Just saying. I think a conversation needs to happen here."

Just then, a roar from the patrons rent the air. One of the college teams got a touchdown, and there was cheering and celebrating drowning out all attempts at conversation, but that was all right. I just needed to think.

I took a sip of my own drink and wondered if I was being a coward.

Chapter 11
Ian

"Ian!"

"You've got to meet Mason. He shreds like a motherfucker! He's a fucking beast!"

Having figured out the tells, I knew it was Finn waving me over as I trotted down the beach with the foam board I'd been renting.

"Hey guys," I called back with an added chin lift.

I dropped my board on the sand next to them and scanned the rolling surf. It always took a second to pull the top half of the thick cold-water wet suit up over my chest and shoulders before yanking on the chord to zip it up my back. The waves looked a little bigger than I was used to, but shit. If the kids were going in, there was no way I was going to chicken out.

For a few seconds, I caught sight of a big guy in

the distance riding the tail end of a wave like a pro. He bailed off the backside just before hitting the whitewash, popping up a few seconds later to grab his board and hop back on. Pointing the nose out to sea again, he paddled out over the swells.

"C'mon," one of the twins said. "Let's join him."

I scowled, torn between wanting to figure this shit out on my own and wanting to get some pointers from the kids. It would be rude to ditch them, and besides, they were good guys along with being Blessing's nephews.

I sighed.

That meant, I was meeting this new guy.

It was Thursday afternoon, the time after school I told the kids I'd meet up with them.

The initial freeze of the water mellowed as I waded into the whitewash before hopping on the board. Pushing the nose of the board down, I dove through an incoming wave before shaking the water off my face and paddling out further. By the time I reached the twins, they were sitting up on their board talking to the guy, Mason.

We looked to be a similar height, and while I knew I was muscular, had good definition from my own exercise, he definitely had me beat. It had to be a hobby or something.

"I thought you came out in the mornings!" the Cody called out to him.

"Problem at the gym." He shrugged, but his eyes

were on me. Shrewdly studying me, even as he added, "I needed to get out here."

"This is Mason. He's with Layla," Finn offered. "He's got a gym in town."

Ah. Now his size made sense. He probably lifted daily while I hit the weights three or four days of the week, depending.

"Ian," I introduced myself once I'd joined them and sat up on my board. "I'm living next door to Blessing."

"And he made the coolest video game," Finn tossed out there. "I was supposed to be studying for my Bio test last night, but I couldn't stop playing. Blessing had to hide all of the game controllers."

The last statement caused the silent man to smirk. Then he was watching me again, this time a hard look in his eyes. "I heard about you."

I nodded, knowing it likely wasn't good.

"There's a good set coming in!" Cody interjected. "C'mon Finn."

I stayed where I was, not breaking eye contact from Mason. We needed to have a conversation. It was there in his eyes. The tension remained thick until the twins took off paddling like mad to catch the next wave.

"Say your peace," I offered.

"What Blessing does is none of my business, but I do feel protective of her."

"Why?" I narrowed my eyes, wondering why he

felt such a personal interest in my girl.

"She's the reason I got to meet Layla. She risked a lot to help my girl leave a dangerous, abusive situation a few years back. That woman is a force for good, and I'll never be able to thank her enough for the impact she's had on my life and Layla's. On that note, I need to give you fair warning. Don't fuck around with her. If you're just looking to fuck someone, find another woman. I won't tolerate anyone's bullshit when it comes to her."

He looked ready to throw down, and while I'd had to do my fair share of fighting in my adolescence, he looked like he might have an edge on me. That wouldn't stop me from doing my best to kick his fucking ass.

Initially, my blood pumped hot, stirred my anger that someone thought they could fucking threaten me. But the longer I stared into his eyes, the more I saw a sincerity there. He was just looking out for her, and could I really be mad about that?

I relaxed my stance, nodded my acceptance. "I hear you, and I'm not out to fuck her over."

"Then what the fuck is this?"

"What," I smirked, "are we talking about our feelings and braiding each other's hair now?"

"Don't be an asshole," he growled, but I could see a brief flash of humor in his eyes. "I want to know that you aren't some fucked up stalker who decided to move in next door."

"Fuck if I fully understand it. Maybe you can tell me," I offered, doing my best to be transparent. "She managed to blow my world apart, make me question everything that I'm doing. She helped me find myself again, and she inspires me. You now? There's something about her."

I stared out over the horizon as my thoughts turned into more of a stream of consciousness.

"I don't know what's happening with me, and I'm not sure what this is yet, but I just need to be around her. A lot. I've never met anyone like her. She's this... this... beautiful, brilliant light that brightens the room when she walks into it, and I don't want to lose that. It felt like...fate. I don't know. The universe. I was looking her up and saw that the apartment was up for sale next to her, and I didn't even think. Just bought it so some other guy couldn't. That's the best I can give you right now. I'm hoping she'll talk to me again."

When I stopped the rambling flow of words, I saw that he wasn't even fighting the smile creasing his face. I scowled. "What?"

"She's your brilliant light? It's fate?"

I felt that fucking blush heat my cheeks again. "Did I say that?"

"You did, but I'm glad."

"You are?"

"Yeah. I'm glad I'm not the only guy who isn't afraid to sound as whipped as you are. Layla's got my number. I can say that for sure."

"Blessing thinks I'm only interested in her game."

"You still trying to get her game?" he asked, somewhat more relaxed.

"Have you seen any part of it?"

"No. She keeps that shit under wraps."

That gave me pause. It was exactly what the boys had said. And yet, she'd shown me. She'd taken me into her computer room and let me see her creations. It said something about how she felt about me. Or had felt. At that time. Reverently, I took a breath of the ocean air and shook my head just thinking about it. "It's epic. It's beautiful."

"So you still want her game."

"Not the way you think." I let the movement of the water act as a balm to my heart. "Not for my company. Not now. At this point, I just want to play it because she created it. Mostly, I want the chance to get to know her. She was the draw. She was the reason I moved."

Mason was silent a beat, then nodded. "I'll still kick your ass if you hurt her, but I can appreciate that you're into her. She deserves to have someone in her corner. She's always had everyone else's back. She's good people."

"I know it."

"I wanted to clear the air because if things go the way I think they will, you and I are probably going to have to be friends." There was a smirk on his face before he checked out the incoming swell. Then he looked over at me. "You gonna just sit there?"

He took off, paddling into the wave. I tried but was too late—the wave went by, bobbing me up and down. Looking back toward the horizon, I watched for the next incoming wave and thought about what he'd said. Blessing and Layla were best friends. If Blessing and I were together, which was not likely to happen considering she communicated through rude gestures when we made eye contact now, but in the case that we did, Mason and I would likely spend some time hanging out. He seemed like an interesting guy.

For a few hours, I got knocked around by the waves and learned how insignificant I was compared to the force of an ocean, but it was better than the last time. Too close to the nose, and I pearled. Too far back, and I was knocked off. Each time, I got back on and paddled back out to wait for a wave, happy to experience the discomfort, the exhaustion, the need to push through all that to get to my goal. It was how I did business. It was how I became successful quickly.

But this was easy, just like my job was easy. I knew what to do. I knew how to get better. I could make improvements. Unfortunately, the Blessing situation was fucked in a way I didn't have the first clue how to fix.

So of course, that was the moment I encountered her. It was nearing sunset. She was already out on the roof patio when I went out there to lay out my wetsuit to dry overnight. I'd bought this one instead of renting it, figuring it wasn't that expensive.

I was contemplating buying a board because this felt like a sport that was going to stick. I was far from good, but there was beauty, a sense of awe, and a feeling of freedom when I was out bobbing on the waves. Just as I figured there would be when I'd watched a few days prior.

That was who I was. I was a doer. There was no sense in procrastination. It wasted time.

Confronted with the Catholic school girl outfit, my southern region swelled, but so did my chest, with a feeling of warmth at the sight of her. She was amazing. Of course she helped Layla. I'm not surprised she'd jump into the middle of a dangerous situation to save a friend. She was fierce. She changed lives. Pedro's. Layla's. Mine.

She was sitting at her little bistro table in the fading light. Small lights that were strung around the patio twinkled against the dusky sky.

"Blessing." I said her name because I wanted to taste her name again on my lips.

She looked over her shoulder. There was a defiance there, like she was still angry, but I sensed sadness as well. More in her body posture than anything.

"I heard you had to hide the game controls last night," I offered lightly.

Her eyes narrowed sharply on me. "When did you talk to the boys?"

"Just now. We were out surfing."

She turned away from me dismissively for a moment. "Yeah. I did."

It hurt that she wasn't even looking at me, and for what? What did I really do? I came here to know her. I came here to be part of her world. I was planning on telling her who I was, but she found out sooner than I could have that talk with her.

That's when I started getting mad, so I decided to go back in. I couldn't help the snap in my tone when I said, "Yeah. I've got work to do. Have a nice night."

"See, that's what I don't get!" she huffed, surging out of her chair.

"What's that?" I taunted. "The fact that I apologized for not introducing myself sooner? The part where I told you I was into you. What exactly is the problem here?"

"You joined the dark side, and there's no way I could be with someone who joined the dark side."

"The dark side?" I scowled. "That's what you're hung up on?"

"Yeah. Someone who could make such a cool game decided to give it up for money. I'm disappointed because I thought you had more integrity."

"You think I don't have integrity?"

"That's what I said."

A sudden fury swamped me at the judgement on her face.

So many sacrifices. So many times, I wanted but couldn't let myself have. So many times, I had worked for days at a time, worked to earn my place and find the talent that would help me make more money, let me take care of my mother. So many times, I had to train myself not to let myself want anymore because there was no point to it.

"How fucking lonely it must be up on your goddamn bourgeoise high horse, Blessing. Let me tell you about my fucking integrity. It includes a breast cancer diagnosis involving my mother. My single mother, who was a housekeeper with no medical insurance who worked her ass off to take care of me, and a son with no fucking money because we grew up poor."

She looked suddenly stricken, but it didn't stop me. My fatigue and frustration sliced the air between us as I drew closer.

"What I did have was a graduate degree, earned through scholarship money, loans, and hard-fucking-work, and an amazing opportunity to start work with a paycheck that would help pay for chemo. I didn't have the fucking luxury of sitting back and following my dreams. Luxury, Blessing. You have experienced fucking luxury."

I made a point of turning a full circle dramatically, my arms wide to illustrate my point before lasering in on her face again.

"I needed to make money to save my mothers' life. That's the story of my integrity. Tell me, how many times have you had to decide between your dreams and someone else's life? Instead, you get to judge me from your pedestal up on the mountain top and play fucking Robin Hood and save the day for others without thinking about it because there is no sacrifice in it for you. So enjoy your ride off into the sunset and leave me to the dark side, as you accused. It looks like I'll be better off there without you."

I could still remember the helpless feeling, at the end of the day, seeing a clump of my mother's hair on the floor. Another in the shower. More in the bathroom trash. Her eyes shimmering with tears at the same time that she firmed her lips up, refusing to give in to the illness.

Fucking badass woman. My mother.

The injustice of it all burned hot and bright in my soul. I'd worked my ass off all my life, and still, I had Blessing looking down her nose at me. For fuck's sake. Why did it hurt when she did it?

Chapter 12
Blessing

Okay. I was officially a bitch, but he fucking called me Robin Hood? Really?

Fine. I deserved it.

Freaking soul assassin. Judgy. Bitchy. Just call me Bitchy McBitchington.

And he was right. It wasn't hard to help people when you had an abundance.

Fuck. I needed to apologize.

A heavy sigh made my chest deflate and Kraken lifted his head from my feet to cock his head up at me. So damn cute. I'd been sitting dejectedly at my computer monitor for the last twenty minutes replaying the conversation that had happened out on the patio. There was no other way to see it.

"I fucked up, Krak," I sighed, and he cocked his head the other direction, trying to understand what I was telling him. I reached out to run my fingers over his soft ears, giving him a quick scratch behind one of them.

He licked my hand, and it didn't even bother me. How weird was that. Maybe I needed to take him to the vet and get him his shots already. It didn't look like he was going anywhere. I was becoming addicted to his unconditional support and soft brown eyes. Even when I did something stupid, he didn't judge. I could learn from him. And, if I was going to keep him, I needed to be fully on-board with his doggy health.

A sigh, self-incriminating, and much deserved, whistled from between my lips as I kept talking to my furry minion.

"I was getting all judgy with him, and he didn't really deserve that. I attacked his integrity. I mean, what kind of asshole does that? This kind, that's who," I muttered, seeing the hurt look on Hulk's face again in my flash of memory. Had his mother survived? Was she okay? Did he have to watch her die?

Shit. That would have had to be horrific. And he'd gone pedal to the metal to make sure he could pay the bills. That kind of diagnosis could have been an immediate death sentence for someone without insurance. He made sure that was not the case.

There was nothing wrong with his ethics or his

integrity, but maybe there was something wrong with mine.

At some point, I was going to need to put on my big girl panties, march on over there, and tell him that I recognized I was being a huge jerk. Not now. No. Right now, I needed to duck my head in shame. Wallow in it. Saturate myself in it until I couldn't stand it anymore.

The pity party is strong with this one, I thought to myself in my internalized Obi-Wan voice.

In an effort to hide from feeling the full force of my shame, I worked through the night. Worked on clarity and color, polishing what was going to become the final product. I gave special attention to the details, to the individual tendrils of hair on the heads of the characters, making sure it looked natural with their movements from my last installment of drawings. I'd even gone back to do quality control of light and shadow around the leaves in the maize, making sure even the veins of the leaves were clearly distinct.

Then I went back to the code. Tried to look at it. Tweak it here and there, to figure out why the hell this fucking glitch persisted. It was around the time the boys woke up for school that I realized I was no closer to fixing the problem than I had been before. And, in fact, I might have made things fucking worse.

I wanted to scream my frustration. If I hadn't

been ready to sob and sleep at the same time, I might have. P-dog. That's who I needed to talk to. But I didn't have the energy for any conversation. Between my mopey guilt from seeing that I'd been the jerk in this scenario and being fruitless in fixing what was wrong with my work, I just didn't have it in me.

The boys left for the day, and though I meant to get ahold of Pedro, I crashed out instead. It was a little after two in the afternoon when I finally sat up and looked at the clock wondering if I'd missed my school bus. Did I still owe a book report to Ms. Benning?

Fuzzy.

Feeling hung over. I blinked a few times in the dim light of the room. There were clouds blanketing the sky. I tried to focus. Blinked a few times to clear my eyes. Couldn't see shit. Remembered that I wore glasses and reached to my nightstand where I almost knocked them on the floor with my clumsy attempt to grab them.

Okay.

It was Friday.

At least, according to my phone it was. And there were texts. One from my nephews telling me they were hanging out with their good friends for the night and wouldn't be back until sometime Saturday afternoon. A follow up text came from my sister telling me she was okay with that plan, and a final text came in from Layla.

She'd given up on waiting for me to have lunch in the office and had gone to Zeke's to have lunch with Mason. She told me to come by if I got myself out of bed at a decent time. Of course, she didn't actually define what "decent" might be. Still, it gave me something to do. I couldn't see getting back in front of my computer just yet.

And so, my place was empty. Quiet. For the first time, it felt strange, so I grabbed some jeans and a sweatshirt. It wasn't a day I was feeling particularly creative about my self-expression. Had I really questioned Ian's integrity?

Yup.

Fuck.

I needed to build some courage. It was time for me to seek out my friend and ask for her help. I probably could use a good mental ass-kicking.

It wasn't quite happy hour by the time I arrived at the club, but clientele was building. Bethany was working. She tipped her head in a casual greeting on her way to a table with drinks, and I mimicked her response. I couldn't see Layla at any of the tables, but it still felt better being here than being alone back at the pad. I grabbed a small bistro table in the corner and hopped up on the stool.

A mule was sounding good. That and some water. I'd have to figure out some food.

"If you're looking for Mayla, they're in the

office." Bethany appeared in front of me, looking as effortlessly elegant as anything. A feminine V-neck T-shirt with gently scalloped, floral-embroidered edges, showed off her girls, which were spectacular. Her signature low rise jeans hung on her hip bones.

I'd never see her have a bad fashion day.

Where did this girl shop? We were going to have to talk, which might mean I would have to be open to getting along.

She dropped a napkin on the table and set a water on it. Her expression was no-nonsense, but there was a look of fatigue there, as well. Not that she was the sharing type. I could relate. Okay. It was happening already. I was empathizing.

"Mayla?" I arched a brow in some confusion and glugged a mouthful to ease the dryness in my throat. Who the hell was that, and why would she think I cared?

"Mason and Layla. It was either that or Layson."

I smirked, appreciating the thing she was doing. Nodded my respect.

"Anyway, they needed to 'talk'," she air quoted, "and disappeared about half an hour ago."

"Code for sex?"

"Absolutely."

We eyed each other for another second before I had to shake my head. "I think I like you in spite of it all. I didn't want to, but there you have it."

"Normally I wouldn't explain myself to anyone,"

she said with a deep inhale, again meeting my gaze in all seriousness.

"Normally, I wouldn't want to hear it."

"My past self would have just called you a bitch and moved on."

"I would have said you're a ho and called it good."

Her lips trembled on a sudden grin that wanted to break free.

I bit my lip, trying to fight it.

"Bitch."

"Ho."

We both started chuckling.

"Glad we got that out of the way." She took a breath and glanced out over the patrons, her eyes taking on a more distant look. "Look, I've been a mess for a long time, and it put me in a bad headspace for a while. I told Layla this but seeing as how we, you and I, may be seeing each other more often because we're both friends of Layla's, I want you to know that I have a lot to apologize for. Mason was always good to me, and I'm so glad he has her. She lets him feel good, and I was too needy to see anyone else's needs but my own."

"She does make him feel good. Maybe she could give me some advice, aside from all the magic pussy therapy she's giving him."

"I'm trying to determine if I should be grossed out by what you just said," Bethany cringed and shook it off. "So why do you need her advice? Did you fuck something up?"

"I did." I lifted the glass of water to press the cold edge to my heated cheeks. "Said some shitty things to someone I was hot for."

"Why would you do that?"

"I was freaked out."

"Because you liked him so much?"

"Maybe."

"So, what magic do you think Layla can give you?" She crossed her arms, her order pad sticking up above her boobs, as she leveled me with a sharp look that wouldn't allow me to get away with anything.

It made me scowl.

"Okay, don't ruin our kumbaya moment with a bitchy attitude."

Bethany rolled her eyes. "We'll never have a kumbaya moment. Neither of us is that girl. Trust me. I'm just saying this isn't rocket science. If you fuck up, you need to own it. Go apologize. Face it. Take your damn medicine. Don't be a baby."

"Okay. That's harsh."

"But honest."

"Yeah, whatever." But I said it with a sigh. "Maybe you are right."

"Thoughtful. Real. Genuine. And if he tells you to fuck off, then you fuck off."

I rubbed my eyes and shoved my glasses back up

my nose. "Yeah. That's what could happen."

"Be brave. Just go do it. Like a hot wax strip. You don't do that slowly. You fucking rip that shit off like a badass, right?"

"Right. Like hot wax." I shuddered, remembering the last bikini wax appointment I'd had before switching to laser hair removal. "That shit hurts."

"If you fucked up..." she shrugged.

I squinted at her. "All right. All right. Okay. So, when did you get to be Dr. Phil?"

She didn't even hesitate. "Shut up and go do what you need to do. You got this. Just tell yourself that."

"Shake a leg, Princess. Orders are piling up," Magnus barked from the kitchen. I could see he was glowering at her over her shoulder.

Again, without blinking an eye or even turning around, she held up a single-digit, silent response over that same shoulder as she continued talking to me. "Report back once it's done, unless you end up balling him all night. I do not need to know that shit. Unless it's kinky. And really good. Then I want full-coverage details. Video if you've got it."

"You are a kinky one, my new friend." I smirked. "Now I know I like you. We might actually become friends."

She gave a short genuine smile. "I better get back to work before He-man decides to have a hissy fit."

Another rude exchange titillated the air between Bethany and Magnus, but I was heading back to the pad and missed the actual words.

What I didn't miss, though, was a slick-looking guy lingering in front of my building a few minutes later. Nice suit. Expensive. Handsome in a clean-cut, boy-next-door kind of way. He was eyeing the store front that was vacant. There'd been a coffee shop under me for a short time, but it hadn't lasted. Parking this close to the beach sucked, and there was an easier café to frequent just a few blocks inland.

As all other pedestrians were doing, I ignored him and walked by him toward the rear of the building. Imagine my surprise when he followed.

"Hey," he called out as I pulled out my keys to unlock the back door. "Are you Blessing Mendoza?"

The hair on the back of my neck rose, and I looked back at him, narrowing my eyes. My keychain had pepper spray, so I palmed it and faced him. Instead of responding to his question, I asked back, "Who are you?"

He put on a well-practiced, but fake, grin and held out a hand to shake as he approached. As an artist, I was well aware of the number of muscles it took to create an authentic facial expression, and he wasn't using half of them. This was a sales job.

"Josh Henderson. Gamecon. Have you heard of us?"

"What do you want?" I ignored his hand, choosing instead to keep my pepper spray handy. He saw that and gave an uncomfortable chuckle before pulling his hand back.

"If you're Blessing Mendoza, then I think we have a lot to talk about."

"Why would that be?"

"Well," he shrugged what was likely supposed to be a non-threatening "golly-gee" kind of gesture and ran a nervous hand over his smoothed back, dirty-blond hair. "I'm the new boss over at Gamecon, and I think you might have something we're interested in buying."

"*You* are the boss?" I arched a brow at him, cocking my head. "What happened to Ian?"

"He's working for me now." There was an arrogance to his statement, a gleeful sneer that was turning him instantly ugly and ghoulish despite giving the impression of being young and hip with his stupid hair and fitted suit. What the fuck was he even wearing?

"Somehow I doubt that," I laughed, which made him flush. He didn't look so charming anymore.

"We just did a big shake-up at the company, and I'm trying to get a handle on all of our talented designers," he pushed, that sneer now directed at me.

"Yeah, well, I'm not one of your designers." I started heading for the door, but he grabbed my arm to stop me.

"Wait!"

"Back off, asshole!" I growled. "Who the fuck do you think you are, touching me?" And seeing my pepper spray about to go off in his face, he let go just as quickly and held up his hands like he was trying to soothe a wild animal.

Damn straight. I was about to kick him in the gonads just for the fun of it. Someone like Ian worked for *him*? No fucking way. I was highly insulted on Ian's behalf with that statement. And if it was true, Hulk was going to hear from me.

"Any contract you have with Ian is now my property, so…"

"Do you know anything about my game, Jerk Face?" I asked, squinting at him.

"My name is Josh."

"No, it's Jerk Face if you want me to keep talking to you. Answer the damn question."

"Well, no. I don't know anything about your game now, but I want to change that."

"Then how do you know my game is good for your company?"

"Ian has a good eye for these things. If there's one thing I can count on, it's that anything Ian has courted has turned to gold." He tried smiling again. "Given his track record, I think you'll be pleased with our offer, once we've seen what you've got."

"And he didn't tell you about it?"

"Well, no, he keeps things pretty close to his chest."

"With good reason, Jerk Face." I laughed and shook my head. "Sorry to waste your time. I've never signed any contract with your company."

"I don't believe you."

"Kiss my ass, Voldemort. Have a nice day."

"*Josh*," a deep voice rasped behind me sounding mean. "I thought I heard you out here."

My Hulk was standing there, a bag of groceries in his thick arms. He'd obviously just come from Pappy's on the corner. "What are you doing here."

"Taking over your accounts." His gleeful sneer was back. His whole attitude taunting and ugly. "You might want to tell your girl here that she's now property of Gamecon."

Ian looked at me and shook his head. "She's not."

"You couldn't close the deal?"

"I didn't want her to have to deal with a shit for brains like you."

Josh's cheeks suddenly flushed violently. "You're going to regret that. I'm taking over all of your contracts. You work for me now."

Ian's smile was decidedly unfriendly. "Oh, but I don't. And never will. I put in my two weeks' notice at the same time I put in for two weeks of vacation. Effective as of two days ago. Now, unless Blessing wants to take a meeting with you, you need to get the hell out of here before you get hauled away for trespassing. You're on private property now."

Josh's lips thinned.

"Wait, so you didn't want my game for your company?" I cocked my head.

"Not if I wasn't going to be in charge of your contract. This guy's a prick. I wouldn't trust him not to fuck you over. That was never my intention. I wouldn't do that to you."

"So you no longer want any part of it?"

"I want to play it. I think it's amazing, and I've only seen a fraction of it."

I looked over at Josh and felt my frustration come out at this whole situation. "Why are you still here? I have not and would never be part of your company. You need to leave."

"You think you can get your game out to the right distributors without our help? Believe that I'll do everything in my power to make sure you're dead in the water. Call me when you're ready for a meeting."

I rolled my eyes. "Cue the evil laugh track. Got it. Now beat it."

Josh stalked off, pulling his phone out of his pocket, as he rounded the corner.

"Glad he's gone," I huffed, turning back to Ian.

He shook his keys out absently, pulling up the one for the door. He was no longer looking at me. It was like an arctic breeze suddenly blew between us bringing a distant look to his face, like he wasn't really seeing me anymore.

That hurt. There was a pinching sensation in my chest. I lifted my hand to rub at it.

He got the door open and tossed over his shoulder, "Yeah, well, good luck with your game. Let me know when it's ready."

"Wait! That's it?"

"That's how we roll on the dark side," he said, a bite to his words and slammed through the door. I was about to get real mad until I pumped the brakes and thought about this whole moment. He was right to throw that shit back in my face. It was meant to be hurtful, and I hurt him.

Well, damn it all anyway. Motherfucking shit.

What the ever-loving-fresh-hell was going on with me?

And he just up and leaves without another word? Unbelievable.

But was I surprised? No.

Did I care? Hell yes.

And he really wasn't part of the evil empire, he really had been looking out for me. Impressed with me. Into me for my body and my brains.

Fucking hell, Batman. You did an expert job of fucking this up.

I needed to make this right.

But how was I going to do that?

I made a quick beeline to my apartment, took ten minutes to change into my best armor—that Catholic school girl costume—with clothing that no schoolgirl would ever be able to step foot on any campus while wearing. He needed my apology, but maybe this would grease the wheels.

And I had to own this, but it didn't mean I couldn't be fierce while doing it.

Chapter 13
Ian

My fucking dick had a mind of its own.

The moment I heard her voice behind the building, I thought about her hand squeezing and rubbing my cock in the hallway. Again. That was all it took for the monster to swell up. Even after the shit she'd said to me. Even with the sting I still felt from her accusations.

Telling me I'd sold out.

Telling Kraken I wasn't her Hulk and someone else would be.

Fuck that. We were going to have some words. I could guaran-fucking-tee her on that. She was acting like an overprivileged brat, and it would be my honor to tell her that as I paddled her ass. Just flip up her little schoolgirl skirt she'd worn yesterday.

The image of that. Fuck.

I could bend her over. Have that pretty ass hiked up in the air just waiting for me to plow right into it. Make her come over and over until her voice was hoarse from the explosions of pleasure.

Not her Hulk.

Of *course* I was her fucking Hulk. She was my Blast. She was the blessing that prompted me to blow up my life and realize that it was a fucked-up existence at this point.

But not if she didn't want me here.

Even if being with her had felt so right.

Why was I even thinking about her anymore?

What I needed to do was sell this place and head back home. Lesson learned. Except, I wasn't sure where that was anymore. No job. And the thought of actually leaving this place left me unsettled. It didn't feel like the right move. The view of the ocean, the feel of the water under my board, the smell of the fresh air was all addicting.

But staying meant I needed to keep facing that sorceress.

The witch next door.

She wasn't shy about putting hexes on me. She needed to take this one back, and we could go our separate ways. Maybe then I could figure out what to do with my life. Forget about her.

But I didn't want to actually leave her. I didn't want to forget about her. I didn't want her out of my system. And yes, I knew this sounded crazy. Even to my own ears. This was what my life had become. Right here. Chaos replacing all of my careful control.

A violent banging on the door reverberated throughout the room. Loud. Pissed off.

It was her. Adrenaline revved me up again. The anticipation was rich. It was time. We were going to have it out. She'd picked a bad time to come over because I wasn't going to be gentle anymore. She was going to hear some things.

"What do you want?" I asked in a flat tone as I opened the door, partially blocking the entrance, ready to confront her with some cold, hard facts about the way she'd been acting.

Blessing stood there defiantly, flushed with emotion, her hands on her hips, ready to confront me. Then I took in what she was wearing.

Fuck me.

She'd put on that Catholic schoolgirl costume. My goddamn kryptonite. Button-up shirt that was tied under her tits, tits that were barely contained inside her low-cut top. Bare legs came out from under her very short plaid skirt. Pig tails? Fucking pig tails. I was not going to last long.

She'd pulled out the big guns.

Goddamn she was beautiful. Full of passion. All it took was one look at her, high color on her cheeks, blue eyes throwing sparks, and I was ready to go caveman on her. Throw her over my shoulder and shackle her to my bed until she started being reasonable. Seeing her long legs with those white knee length socks was killing me. Imagining them wrapped around my hips had the monster getting thicker and heavier, pushing to break free of the denim.

She just did it for me. And she fucking pissed me off like no other.

What panties was she wearing?

"You make me crazy!" she hissed, ignoring my bulk. She pushed through, shoving past me, to march inside my apartment uninvited, before spinning around to confront me, hands on her hips.

"I make *you* crazy?" I barked a laugh that held no humor and slammed the door as I turned to face her.

There was satisfaction in that microaggression since I couldn't just hike her little skirt up and grab her ass. This woman, who had me all twisted up in knots, was accusing me of confusing her life? She had no idea.

"Yes!"

"Well, how about this." I crossed my arms across my chest to keep from reaching for her, but my jaw felt tight as I said, "I've known you for like five fucking minutes, and now you're all I think about. What you're up to. How to get you over here. How to keep you here. How to get inside your goddamn skin."

"My panties?" she asked with an imperious tilt of her chin.

"Always," I growled, my voice coming out rough. "I love your little panties. I think about getting into your pretty little panties every minute of the fucking day. But I also want more from you. Much more."

"That's what I'm talking about!" she hissed. "That right there!"

"What?"

"Right there!" Blessing stuck an accusatory finger out at me, her "mad kitten" look in full effect, tits bouncing with her arm movements, almost spilling out of her shirt. "You get me all hot and bothered with all of your man muscles and sexy times fantasies running through my head, and then you get me all hot and bothered even *more* with all your sexy talk about your fucking genius video game and getting to know each other more, and I start thinking maybe there's something here because that has never happened to me before. I don't get emotional over guys. Never. Ever. But look at me!"

She raised her hands in supplication to the universe.

I was looking all right, especially with her nipples almost busting free, her little scrap of a white lacy bra pushing them up and out.

She was also starting to say some of the right

things, and my heart swelled with warmth.

But she wasn't finished with her rant.

"I'm a freaking freak coming at you like this, being a big old dick when I don't even have a dick! I'm all confused and weird and anxious because I like you, but I don't want to like you, and it scares me! Okay? I don't do serious, but not because I don't want to. Layla is looney over her man, and I tease her about it, but it's either that or feel jealous because secretly, I want to have those feelings."

"Are you done yet, little Blast?" I prowled closer. Fuck, she was hot in a schoolgirl uniform. Was I going to get to flip that damn little skirt up after all?

"No! I'm not. You actually fucking moved into my building and for what? Why? I was normal before I met you. At least, normal for me. I understood my life and could predict what I was going to do day by day, but now I stand in a room for ten minutes suddenly realizing I don't remember why I walked into it because I'm so goddamn busy thinking about you! Worried about you! Feeling like a P.O.S. because I hurt you, which is not like me at all! Fuck!"

"What did you come here for?" I interrupted, moving in on her, letting her know she had my full, undivided attention. "Looking like a present I want to unwrap. Did you think I would just look past everything and jump you?"

"I'm trying to fucking tell you that I'm sorry for the bullshit I said the other day, and while I had every right to be mad at you for keeping your identity from me, I had no business being a judgy bitch to you. I was just so mad because I was seeing you with stars in my eyes as my own personal Hulk, and then my feelings got hurt, so I lashed out. And I'm so sorry. I was hurtful, and I don't want to hurt you. And if you tell me to fuck off now, I will because I would deserve it." She looked down at her hands, which were twisting nervously in the material of her short little skirt.

"Did you think it would go over better if you sexed me up?" I narrowed my eyes, frowning down at her. I wasn't sure if she could see the smile that was trying to break free.

"Maybe." She finally looked up at me, scowling. "Yeah. Did it work?"

"Are you finished with your apology now?"

"Yes. No. I don't know. It depends." She was still wearing her cute little scowl, but underneath it all, I could see the uncertainty.

"On what?"

"You're response."

"My response?" Fuck. This girl...

I closed in on her instantly. With one hand cupping the back of her head to hold her in place, and the other grabbing her ass under her skirt, I molded her to my body, folded myself around her, let myself sink into her sweet, plump lips. It was like coming home. I devoured them, slanting to deepen the feel of her, savored not only the soft gasp and long, drawn-out moan that vibrated between us like the best music, but her sweet taste that I couldn't get enough of. I was starving for her. Dominating her with my size and strength.

But this was Blast, a girl who took what she wanted, and she wanted to do her own damage. She curled a leg around my thigh. Grabbed my ass to pull me closer. Teased my cock with her sweet little grind that she was so good at. And with my hand running back up her leg from its position on her round cheek, I held her thigh in place, up high, spread open for me. She was giving my cock teasing reminders of the heaven that awaited him between her legs, reminders that he belonged inside of her hot, wet center, and that was when the slow simmer erupted into a wildfire.

Our tongues rubbed together as the kiss deepened, and the desperation mounted. A blast of heat shot straight to my dick, had it pulsing thick and hard, like granite, with an ache that was demanding release after days of being left unsatisfied, teased beyond what was bearable where this woman was concerned. The burning need was relentless.

Her arms crossed tightly behind my neck, my sexy little Blessing moaned her pleasure in soft, mewling cries. They were the most erotic sounds, and they were driving me insane. I needed to get between her legs.

I picked her up, both my hands on her curvy, bare ass under her skirt at the same time her legs wrapped around my hips like they had a mind of their own, my cock rubbing against her little pussy through my denim fly, driving both of us to need more. I set her down on the barstool a few feet away, kept her legs spread wide, straddling my hips. Continued my own slow grind, the monster growing harder with each thrust, and had her breaking away from our kiss, panting with her own mindless pleasure. I let the monster tease her. Torture her. Keep her on edge.

She deserved it after the week she put me through. To that end, I slowed my grind, took away some of her friction, and grinned wickedly when she gave a protesting sound.

"You owe me, little Blast. What are you going to do to make this better?" The steely words were a rumbling demand by her ear. She was required to make amends, and she liked it, judging from the heated look she gave me when I pinned her with my eyes.

"What would you like me to do?" she asked breathlessly.

"Unbutton your top two buttons," I demanded. Her fingers were trembling when she reached for the first.

As each button was undone, more of her sweet, plump flesh was revealed. Her candy-pink nipples became visible through the sheer, white lace of her bra, just waiting for my mouth. Hooking a finger in each bra cup, I pulled the lace aside just enough to let her nipples pop free.

"Beautiful," I said gruffly, rubbing them between my fingers, both at the same time, and she cried out harshly, a raw sound, gasping each breath.

"Feels so good, Hulk," she breathed tremulously, a plea in her eyes to keep going.

"Prettiest fucking sight. So fucking responsive." I owned that look of desire. Wanted to bring it to fruition. Make her explode with it.

"French kiss them," she panted another breath.

"I've been wanting to do this for a long time," I muttered.

Then I was sucking and kissing one pebbled nipple, her moans of pleasure spiking the air with sultry sounds of stark need. It was pure animal, the things I wanted to do to her, the ways I wanted to make her scream my name. Not wanting to be neglectful, I suctioned onto the other pretty, swollen tip, needing to leave some part of myself on her skin. Flicking and scraping with my teeth, I kept up the assault until her hips were rocking against my aching cock.

"Oh shit," Blessing cried out, her fingers

threading through my hair to keep my mouth in place. "That feels so good. So good."

All she could do was hold on, gasp each cry of pleasure, and demand I keep going, while rubbing her pussy against me for some much-needed friction.

"Want me to make you come this way? I could do it," I threatened, the sight of her candy pink nipples, all shiny and hard from the attention my lips and tongue gave them, making me feel like they were mine. Claimed. Owned. Her orgasm was going to be mine. Everything about her was mine. Fucking mine. Finally.

"I need to feel you inside of me," she breathed heavily, her pale eyes heated and hungry. As though she couldn't help herself, she leaned in to take more, capturing my lips again, nipping and sucking. She was reaching for the monster, cupping him through my jeans. Rubbing at him. He'd never been so fucking engorged.

I had to still her hand, trapping it under my own, before this ended too fast.

She wanted me, maybe as much as I wanted her. She'd driven me crazy for days, where all I could think about was getting my hands on her. Fucking blue balls for days. And it was deliberate. She'd been trying to get me going.

"You've had him hard all week," I growled.

"He needs special care. Can the monster come

out and play?" she asked, her words a puff of air against my lips.

What a fucking sight. Her nipples playing peekaboo with her bra that got shoved aside, her skirt pushed up to her hips with her little white panties peeking out because her legs were spread wide enough to fit my hips. When I slid fingers toward her center, I felt the silky material. It was soaked, and she was on edge. Trembling. An involuntary moan shuddered through her at my touch.

"Only if you make him feel welcome. His feelings have been hurt."

"I can take care of him." She looked up at me, her eyes hungry, glazed over with lust, and gave him a squeeze that had me groaning and gritting my teeth to keep from coming.

"How?" I asked

"I could give him a kiss." She leaned in again, sucked on my lower lip. Nipped at it.

"He'd like that," I said roughly, brushing my own lips over hers, back and forth. Making promises.

"French or regular?"

"You and your French."

"It's the best."

"Holy fuck, Blast. You're going to make him blow his load, and you haven't even touched him yet."

"Set me down, and I can start making him happy again." She even licked her lips, like she was anticipating something delicious. A fresh surge of need targeted my cock, and I groaned with the overwhelming pleasure/pain of it, already spewing precum. I needed to get him under control.

"I think we can do better than this."

"Bedroom?"

"Bed." I pulled her off the barstool and carried her down the hallway. Turning to shove the door wide with my shoulder, I flicked on the light and tossed her on the bed before skewering her with a hungry look. "But don't think this gets you out of anything. We have things to talk about."

"I know we do."

"But for now, we fuck."

"We fuck," she agreed, her words sounding beautifully needy.

"Hard and good," I commanded.

"Oh my God, yes," she nodded rapidly, her blond pigtails swaying with her movement. I was going to need to do something with those. Grab them. Pull on them. Hold her in place while I made her come a few times.

"What do you think of my response?" I'd circled back to her earlier statement.

"Exactly what I wanted," she breathed out shakily.

"Except for one thing."

"What's that?"
"You're wearing far too many clothes."

Chapter 14
Blessing

Turned out, he didn't want me to take my clothes off at all.

He ran his large, rough hands up my white, knee-high socks after tossing me down on the bed, and kneeling between my spread legs. Did I mention that I loved being manhandled? Tossed around? He was just the guy to do it.

It got me going like nothing else. I could feel how dripping wet I was.

"Leave this on. You are a goddamn feast."

Ian's voice was a low rumble, his vibrant jewel-toned eyes that couldn't decide if they were blue or green, eyed my body like it was about to be his next meal.

He reached down, spread my shirt open wider and pull the cups of my bra further down to frame up my breasts more fully. I loved seeing the fierce hunger in his eyes when he ran his big, knuckles over the hard tips muttering "fucking beautiful" and "these are mine", but he left my skirt in place, muttering, "Want to be able to flip that skirt up and find your bare ass when I flip you over. Been fucking driving me insane since I first saw you in it."

"That was the point."

"Oh yeah?" He settled his weight on me, and it felt perfect. Everything felt perfect. It felt right. The way he looked at me, touched me. More tingles, more heat, more skin, more kisses, more tongue, more tasting. It was so good, I wanted everything all at once.

Then he was pushing my skirt up with his big man hands, his thumbs edging the elastic of my silky thong right where I was wettest, most needy, and my thoughts scrambled.

"Yes, baby," I whispered and sucked in air, my hips rising to meet his touch.

His eyes met mine, warmed at the endearment. Then he was angling his head to watch his thumb run a light path over that highly sensitized hotspot, the gentle touch, too gentle, frustrating me with tingles of heat that ramped up my need even more. "You are soaked, little Blast."

"Please," I whimpered. "I need your fingers there. Inside me. Please, Hulk!"

But an evil grin suddenly emerged, and I knew I was in trouble.

"You were a bad girl, Blast. Weren't you the girl who was flipping me off for a couple of days?" he squinted down at me, let his magical thumb edge the elastic again, barely easing underneath to steal a quick caress over my swollen, wet lips, before backing out again.

More slick arousal pulsed between my legs.

"No. I'm sure that was someone else," I protested. "Touch me."

"Are you certain?" he asked again, that dangerous thumb slipping up under my panties to tease and torment for yet another brief swipe before pulling away again. I growled at him, scowling my frustration.

Fuck, he had me in a corner.

"Okay, fine. If that was me then I totally apologize. Touch me, Hulk!"

"Oh, Blast. I thank you for your apology." Then he brushed his thumb over my wet panties, rubbing over me with a precision that had me crying out, trying to grind on his hand.

Fuck. I loved his fingers. Thick and strong. But they pulled back again, and I held my breath a second, then panted it out, anticipating where he might let his fingers roam. Just the feel of his hands running over my body at all, clothed or otherwise, was sending a mega pulse of heat between my legs.

I felt the gush of slick arousal at my pussy and couldn't stop the moan that parted my lips.

"I think you like this," he taunted with a hint of a dark smirk on his face. Then he was ripping through the delicate material of my panties, and his fingers were up my skirt, slipping and sliding in the wet heat that oozed from my core. "You're soaking wet. Damn, but I want to feel you squeezing my cock. Right here." He let a finger tap the very place that was feeling so empty.

"Take this off," I demanded, yanking on the hem of his shirt. "I want to feel your skin. I need to trace your muscles with my tongue."

"Not before I French kiss your pretty pussy," he growled, but grabbed a handful of shirt from behind his head and pulled it off anyway.

Just as beautiful as I remembered.

He was all masculine energy with thick, broad muscles that begged to be explored by curious lips, and strength that promised to manhandle me in just the right way. Even his size, being so much larger than me, was a kink I was embracing. I wanted to be his little plaything that he fucked good and hard. Those were the key words here. Good and hard. I wanted to feel it in the morning.

"You say the dirtiest things."

"You inspire me," he smirked. "You asked about the panties I took from you? They're covered in my cum."

"Oh, shit," I moaned at the image, and then it was on. It was all tongue, teeth, and lush, sucking kisses that only fueled the engine.

Ian pressed into my body, his weight trapping me in a way that pushed my wild button. My legs curled around his thighs, and with that movement, my skirt slid upward. His jeans were just the right friction in the right place, and I arched against him with a cry.

A sexy grin curved his lips when he suddenly broke off our kiss, both of us breathing heavily. He kissed his way down my torso and didn't stop until he could pull my skirt up and find my pussy.

"Blessing," he sounded happily tortured. "Fuck. You're bare?" Then his face was between my thighs, and he breathed me, a primitive groan coming from deep in his chest before his lips were on me, working my pussy and clit. Licking and sucking with a precision that had me crying out.

"Yes!" I gasped, grinding on his face some more. "Like that!"

He doubled his efforts, and his finger found its way into my center, adding another layer of sensation and heat. My hips moved on their own, meeting his thrusts, desperate for the orgasm that had been on the brink of sending me tumbling over the edge for the last half hour.

"Your pussy is so damn sweet," he suddenly snarled, still lapping and kissing my juices from my pounding, pulsing core, his big shoulders holding my legs open wide as he feasted like a starving man.

"Oh, my fuck!" I cried out, hardly able to string sensible words together.

"This is mine, Blessing. Mine." His primal growl sent another wave of hot need straight between my legs.

"Yes! Yes!"

He latched on to the bundle of nerves and sucked hard, added another finger, stretching my inner flesh. Then I was there, gasping with the release that quaked pleasure through my body relentlessly.

"Ian! Oh, shit," I panted, his fingers still moving until it was too much, and I pushed at his head.

He languidly gave my pussy another lick before sitting up to scoot off the bed. Before I could question what he was doing, he was back with me, this time, sans pants. He really was a beautiful male specimen. His cock was big and thick to the point of being nearly purple. He was so hard his cock was standing straight up. He knelt on the bed, taking the time to roll on a condom.

The sight of it was enough to get my blood thickening again. As much as my orgasm had felt good, it would feel so much better if he was pounding me.

"I could look at you all day," I admitted from the depths of my orgasmic glow. "You look good. I just want to bite your ass."

"Anytime." With that promise in his eyes, he crawled back up my body, trapping me deliciously for the second time, kissing me, deep and urgent as though he was dying of thirst, and I was his drink of salvation.

Then he was sinking into me, my skirt bunched up around my waist, and his big dick stretching me to the point of burning until pure pleasure took over. He groaned as he got fully seated inside me.

"Fuck, you're so tight and hot. Fucking squeezing me like I knew you would. You okay," he asked, his eyes searching my face at the same time that his teeth were clenched from the raw lust that was ready to take over.

"Better than," I said before moving my hips. "But you need to move. You said hard."

"Hold on, Blast. We're going for a ride."

His body curled around mine, his hands cupping my ass to get as deep as possible. At first, his thrusts were long and deliberate, and his lips found mine again while our hips worked together in this dance. Then he going faster, and he lifted his head. His eyes were burning into mine as we watched each other climb higher and higher. Before long, he was pounding into me, and it was glorious. Each thrust hit a nerve ending that fanned the wildfire sweeping through my body. We were both crying out a chorus of guttural grunts and sharp moans. I met each thrust with my legs wrapped around his hips.

"Are you close," he asked, sweat beading at his temple.

"So close," I whimpered.

"Touch yourself," he commanded, and with my fingers strumming over my clit, and his cock ramming into me, I came like a goddamn champ. Shouting out, my body convulsing around his shaft, my legs shaking. Only then was he grunting each powerful thrust, chasing his own finish, finally giving in to his own release, coming with a guttural half-growling, half-shouting triumph that echoed through the room.

Suspended in time, our eyes clinging fiercely to each other, our gasping breaths mingling between our parted lips, I'd never felt so close to anyone. Ever.

On a final deep breath in, he crashed half over me, his face shoved into my neck. His weight felt good on me, and I held him there, pressed to my heart. Let my hands roam his back and shoulders before cupping his taught, muscled ass. He wasn't the only one feeling proprietary. Involuntarily, his hips ground into mine, his cock still deep inside me. I wanted him there. Intimate. Have him so deep inside me it was hard to know where we were separate.

I wouldn't let myself think about why these

feelings could be scary. Not going there. Not now.

Pressing a gentle kiss to the side of my neck, he rolled to the side to dispose of the condom. Then he was pulling me up against his big, warm body, our legs intertwined, my face on his chest, the comforter pulled over us. We were quiet long enough that I thought he'd dozed off until he suddenly tightened his arm around me.

"Why the name Blessing?" he asked.

Shadows were lengthening in the room. The sun had never made a full appearance through the cloud cover, leaving the room in semi-darkness. I could see enough to know he had bare white walls and the bare minimum of furniture: bed, nightstand, dresser.

"I was unexpected. My parents thought they were beyond their child-rearing years and got drunk and handsy one night. Nine months later, you know, I came along. Fifteen years younger than my older sister. Anyway, they always wanted me to know I was wanted and loved."

"You are a blessing."

I felt the warmth of the compliment and pressed a kiss to his chest. "And it let me know from an early age that my parents were still horny for each other. They still can't keep their hands off each other. I think a lot of kids might have been embarrassed by that, but I was always proud, you know. They were my example."

"Sounds like a solid start." His fingers trailed

over my arm that was spayed across his chest.

"It was. Still, they were older, so I ended up spending a lot of time on my own. Living in my head."

"I like what's in your head. Without that alone time, you might have turned out just like every other kid you knew instead of becoming Batman."

I smirked. "I see you've been talking to Pedro."

"He's loyal. Wanted to kick my ass for hurting you."

I grinned. "He's Spiderman. We were the heroes instead of the weirdos. We all have our norms, right? My norm let me exercise my creativity in ways I might not have otherwise."

"The game."

"Yeah." Thinking about where Pedro and I were in it had tension tightening up some of my muscles. Were we ever going to figure out the glitch? Added to that, I hadn't really worked on it much the last few days. I pulled away just the slightest bit, but he noticed the shift.

"What is it?"

"I'm just…stressing." I pulled away more, leaning back onto my own pillow, thinking about where I'd left off on it, no closer to solving our problem than before. And Pedro couldn't figure it out. If anyone could, he could. But he couldn't. At least not yet. I was afraid of discovering that it would become a "not ever" status change.

Then I would be fucked.

"It takes a lot to put a game out there."

"Yeah. Years. Heart and soul. Sweat and tears. I worked on it solo for ten years. The art was always there in my mind, the story. Of course, the world I wanted to live in was growing more complex as I got older. I trained more in computer graphics to try and meet the need. So many classes. Pedro's team joined me on this goal almost three years ago. There were more complex things I didn't have the skills to code, and he's a genius with this stuff."

"Sounds like you should be about done."

"Yeah, well, it is at this point. We'll be fine. I know it. There's just been this persistent...glitch. But we'll get past it soon."

His eyes widened, like I'd surprised him.

"What?"

His lips quirked, and he bent to kiss my forehead before leaning back on his pillow again. "'Glitch.' It's funny that you would use that word. I've been using it to describe some of the personal life choices I've made."

"Glitch?" I asked, smiling up at him. "Like, you have personal glitches?"

"Exactly." He took a deep breath. "You don't know me well, but this hasn't been the usual me. The way I've been the last few months is not me. I'm different than this."

"What do you mean?" I leaned up on my elbow

to better see his face, appreciate the sharp lines of his jaw and cheekbone. The blanket fell away, and he took a moment to lust after my breasts that were still playing peekaboo with my wonderfully slutty bra and shirt.

Good.

My fingers couldn't help tracing a path along his more masculine bone structure. He turned his head to kiss my wandering fingers, capturing me with his pretty eyes again. Their brilliant shade surrounded by dark lashes. Why did men always get thick, full lashes?

He lifted his head to slide one of his forearms behind it as a prop, muscle bulging in that position, and resettled himself on it. Distracting as hell, but I fought the desire and refocused.

"From the first moment I knew about you, I started down a whole different path, like I hit this unexpected fork in the road telling me that it was time to do something different."

"Like spontaneously move?"

"Right."

"Quit your job?"

"Exactly. I've been working toward one end so long, I haven't known any other way to be. It's like I've been on this treadmill that's been set at full speed, and I didn't even realize I could get off."

"You were taking care of your mom."

"Yeah. Maybe on some level, I was associating

her health with my work, so I couldn't let myself stop."

"She's healthy now?" I asked tentatively, still feeling like a shit for the things I'd said. "Cancer free?"

"Completely."

"I'm so glad. I really am sorry for being such a dick."

"It's all right. You more than made up for it."

He leaned over and gave one of my nipple a French kiss that made my toes curl for a few moments. Then he leaned back on the cushion of his arm, a knowing look in his eye from hearing me suck in a breath. That was an evil move. One I might have to learn.

My pussy clenched with glee.

She was going to have to wait.

"She's been clear for a couple of years now. But there were moments of abject fear."

I nodded, took a breath, and tried to ignore the new throb happening between my legs.

"Maybe you aren't different. Maybe you're just finding your way back to your original path?"

He was quiet a moment, gazing up sightlessly at the ceiling before a wide grin touched his beautiful lips. When he laid that one on me, my heart grew two more sizes. Just like the Grinch.

"I like your explanation better. I'll go with that. So, what's going on with your glitch."

"It's just a thing. I mean, I keep feeling like we have it handled, but it's frustrating. I thought we'd be finished by now. We've been in the testing phase for a long time trying to figure this problem out. I wanted to be done long before Comic Con in San Diego."

"You have a panel scheduled?"

"I'm planning to. We'll launch it at Comic Con with test models ready to go. This feels like we're cutting it close. We also needed time to raise some capital, but you can't attract investors if you can't let them try the product."

"Is there anything I can do? I might not be the artist you are, but coding is my specialty."

"I'm sure we'll figure it out."

There was a small part of me that wanted to take him up on the offer, but the bigger part of me was still protective. My feelings for him were so fresh and new, as yet to be analyzed, and I wasn't ready to turn pieces of myself over to him. It felt like too much all at once. Instead, I turned to face him again, this time with my remorse written on my face.

"I do need to apologize to you. It couldn't have been easy taking care of your mom fresh out of grad school."

"I was terrified. I thought I was going to lose her, and she means the world to me." His eyes shimmered for a moment before he blinked the moisture away. "She lost her hair during chemo. It was hard to watch, and she tried to be so brave, but I heard her crying one time. She was in the bathroom. Thought I couldn't hear. I listened for a moment, then gave her the space she needed to let go without having to deal with me being her witness."

"You had to have felt so helpless." I felt my own heart clench, seeing him relive the pain of it.

"She'd always had long, beautiful hair."

"It was part of her identity?"

"Yeah. She might not have had nice clothes or a nice house, but she'd always been blessed with beauty. Inside and out. Partly to her detriment. My dad took off and never looked back when she was still pregnant with me. He was too busy. Didn't have time for a wife or kid."

"Bastard."

"Pretty much. He's also the reason I never got seriously involved with anyone. The job was my first priority, and I wasn't willing to put a relationship on a backburner. I never wanted to treat a woman that way."

"Did you ever know him?"

"I met him once. Found him. About a year ago."

"You did? Where was he?"

"Car sales. Owned a dealership all this time. Had some money."

"Double bastard!"

"Pretended like he didn't know who my mom was at first, and when I didn't let him bullshit me, he got mad and told me I wasn't getting a dime out of him."

"He thought you were just after him for his money?" The look on my face had to show my abject disgust of such a human.

"Yeah. Imagine his surprise when I got into my Porsche and told him to fuck off. That I could buy his place ten times over and still not feel a dent in my bank account."

That came as its own shock to me. Hulk was rich. I mean, I figured he had something going on, but holy shit. He was super rich.

"Was that the last time you saw him?"

"Yeah. He must have found out about me at some point because he started leaving me messages at the company. But that ship sailed."

"So that brings up the obvious question. What are you going to do now? You don't have a job and you aren't exactly of an age to retire."

"I got an offer from VisiStation for the same position I'm in now, but with a hefty raise."

"You still need the money?"

"No." He sighed a breath. "My work over the last five years particularly brought nearly a billion in revenue into the company. I've been well compensated. I don't have to work at all."

"Then why go back and work for some other

jack-off?" My fingers drifted down over the lines created by the muscles in his abs. "Same shit, different assholes."

"But I wouldn't know what to do with myself. This is what I know."

"I'd say, don't rush into anything. Think on what makes you happy and just do that."

"Aren't you the wise one." A frown fell over his face. "I heard you say I wasn't your Hulk anymore."

"I didn't mean it. I was mad."

"Am I still your Hulk?"

"No one else has ever hulk-stomped my door in."

"That's right," he nuzzled my neck. Heated tingles radiated from that spot making my blood thicken and pool once again in sensitive places. "Was that only a week ago?"

"Wait a minute. I said that hulk thing when I was alone. Are you saying you can hear me?" I frowned.

"When you're in the kitchen. It feels like you're right in the same room with me. It's how I heard you the other morning we met. Are you going to be mad about that, too, now?" Then he looked over my face. "You don't seem surprised."

I narrowed my gaze thoughtfully and bit my lip to try and keep from smiling. It didn't work.

"What?"

"I heard you come the last two nights. You said

my name."

His cheeks flushed, but he owned it. "Fuck yeah, I did. Because you hexed me."

"It worked?"

In response, he took my hand and held it to his hardened cock, his aquamarines heating me up with their silent demand. "I've been living in a perpetual state of blue balls since that night."

I pouted my lips in sympathy, but my wicked intent was in my eyes just before giving his swollen dick a good squeeze.

"I can't have that on my conscience now, can I?"

Chapter 15
Ian

"Does the monster want to come out and play?"

As she asked the question, Blessing squeezed my cock which was eagerly swelling, just waiting for her soft little hands to wrap themselves around him. When they did, I groaned with the pleasure of it.

"So good," I hissed as she stroked, her fingers running the length of my cock before she sat up to follow where her hand went.

"I've been wanting to taste you," she murmured. Moments later, she crawled down my body, her hot mouth poised above my cock a second before she kissed the tip. Precum coated the head, and she sucked it off as we both moaned. "I like how you taste, Hulk."

"I'm all yours, baby."

Then she was running her tongue from base to

tip before her lips suctioned over the top, causing scorching pleasure to shoot through me.

"Sexy as fuck," I muttered, watching how my cock was disappearing into her warm mouth, how her hand was spreading her saliva over my shaft while pumping and squeezing me. With my hips jerking to meet the bobbing motions of her head, my dick was tunneling into her mouth. My balls were growing tighter, but it was the sight of her short little skirt playing peekaboo with her ass cheeks that had me pulling her off my cock before I could blow.

"What?" she protested, flushed, her lips swollen and glossy. It was a good look. A "we're-going-to-fuck" look.

"I want to come inside you, Blast. Get on your knees."

She gave me a sexy little smile before doing as she was told. Facing away from me, she got on her knees with her ass in the air, and I finally got to flip her little skirt up and out of the way. Her pretty pink pussy was swollen and wet. Irresistible. Even as I reached to grab a condom with one hand, I had to run my other fingers over her soaking slit, working them into the silken heat of her.

Pushing back into me, she moaned, drenching my fingers with more of her molten heat.

"Look how much your pussy likes me, Blast." I kept moving my fingers inside of her, only pulling out long enough to slide the condom on. Then I was back to pushing the monster inside his own private heaven.

"Ohhhh…" she moaned, feeling the slow thrust of my dick inside of her. Deliberately, I was keeping it slow, savoring each twinge of sensation, denying the drive that prompted me to pound her sweet body into the mattress.

"Your little pussy sucks my cock in, Blast. All the way in. So fucking tight and greedy." I punctuated each thrust, her skirt bunched up in my fists, controlling her through the waistline of the material. I loved grabbing her and putting her exactly where she needed to go.

"Yes, oh fuck, oh yes," she was chanting in a breathless, panting cry, half muffled by the bedding. "I fucking love your cock, Hulk. So fucking good."

Which was just what she needed to say for me to level up. Now I just wanted to take over. Own her. Know that she was my little Bomb Blast, and that this was so fucking good, she would only ever want my cock pounding her sweet little pussy.

I reached for her arm, pulling it behind her back for better leverage, and started pounding into her. Skin slapping, the air was punctuated by her cries and my growls. I reached around to pinch and rub at her clit, and a keening sound of ecstasy was building from deep in her body.

"I'm going to come! Don't stop! Don't stop!

Don't stop!" she cried before she was screaming my name, her pussy clamping down on my dick and milking my orgasm from me even before I wanted to give it up. A white-hot flash of heat exploded within me, and with a final thrust and guttural roar, I filled the condom with cum. I was shaking in the aftermath, my hips still moving inside her warmth, but gentler now.

"I need to get rid of the condom," I panted, my hips finally still, "but I don't want to pull out of you just yet."

"I'm on the pill, and I haven't had sex in more than a year. I'm clean."

"Are you saying we don't need condoms?" I asked, just the idea making my dick perk up, even though he wasn't ready to go again just yet. "I'm clean. I've never gone without protection. Ever."

"I want to feel you inside me next time," she sighed into the covers. She hadn't moved a muscle from where she'd collapsed after coming.

"Fuck, yeah. Next time. Right now, I need to dispose of this."

"Shit. I need to see to Kraken. He usually sleeps with me."

"Bring him here. He can sleep in the living room. There's a nice comfy rug." I spanked her ass to get her moving. She yipped with surprise and rubbed a hand over it.

Blessing pulled herself off the bed with a pout,

and we both made trips to the bathroom to clean up before heading back out to the living room to take care of business. Kraken happily settled his sleepy self on the padding Blessing brought over. She put a bowl of food and water down, which he promptly ate.

"Cold pizza," I announced, handing a slice to her from the fridge.

"Yum," she murmured, munching down on it. "I hadn't eaten anything today."

"We could order something," I offered, finishing off a slice in just a few bites. "Are you hungry for more?"

"Just bed. Really tired."

So that's what we did. Headed back to the bedroom, Kraken got settled on his bed pad, and I pulled the rest of Blessing's clothing off of her. She slid back into bed nude, curled up into me, and promptly fell asleep.

Once in the night, I woke to feel her naked body pressed to mine, her lips sucking on my neck. With her leg thrown over my own, it was easy enough to reach down, feel how wet she was, and slide right in. Body to body, skin to skin, I felt every rise and fall of her chest, the soft puff of her breath with each sound of pleasure she made.

I grabbed her ass to grind each thrust, so her clit was stimulated before she was prompted to climb on top and ride me until we both shouted our release.

This time, we were out for the count.

Chapter 16
Ian

My buzzing phone woke me up.

I was alone in bed, which gave me a moment of panic until I remembered that I knew exactly where Blessing lived. In fact, I would look forward to paddling her ass for leaving me without saying goodbye. Even if she had good reason.

The buzzing stopped.

Her ass was a thing of beauty. Perfect for my hands. Then there were her tits. Perfect for my mouth. Just thinking about all the places on her body that I kissed and touched, all of her holes that I invaded or played with, all the ways that she made me feel weak in the knees, had the monster rising again.

I gave him a casual stroke, pumped him a couple times, like I was commiserating with him. She wasn't here. Then the buzzing started up again. Broke the mood.

With a heartfelt groan, I rolled out of bed and located where the buzzing was happening. I'd left my phone in my pants where I'd dropped them in my hurry to get inside Blessing's hot fucking body last night.

Six missed calls. Three were from Sal. Two were clients and one was the old CEO of Gamecon, Rick Montoya, who'd quit due to medical issues. I had to wonder what he wanted. Before the call ended, I managed to pick up.

"What's going on, Sal?"

"Ian. Fuck." The relief in Sal's voice was obvious. "I know it's Saturday, but the phone has been ringing off the hook. People trying to get ahold of you, and you being unavailable has been fucking crazy."

"Sal, you need to know I put in my two-week notice. Just giving you the heads up."

"Yeah, I know. That's what everyone's talking about. Harvey's calling for you. Josh is trolling all of the clients. The clients are calling, ready to walk away. Everyone wants to talk to you."

"It's why I included an opt-out clause. They can get out, go where they want."

"Chris wants to know if you're out because you're starting your own company now. It's something I want to know, too. If that's happening,

I want to sign up. I'm happy and willing to come south and work for you."

My own company. I let that thought spin out for a minute. What did Blessing say yesterday? Why would I want to work for another asshole doing the same shit? If I had my own company, I could do whatever the hell I wanted.

The idea wasn't making me cringe, in fact, just the opposite. But it was a big step. One that I needed to think on for more than a few minutes.

"To be honest, Sal, I don't know what my next step is going to be."

"You could do it. The phone has been ringing nonstop, and more than half of the calls are clients wanting to follow you. All of our biggest assets are pissed, ready to walk. Guys you found and brought in. Think about it. Seriously. Then hire me. But in any case, Harvey is looking to talk to you."

"I'll give him a call." Mostly I was hoping to finally be able to tell him to go fuck himself.

"Seriously, dude. I might come south and camp out at your place anyway."

"I hear you. Let me wake up and wrap my head around all this."

After ending the call with Sal, I pulled on a pair of athletic shorts, or as Blessing called them, my "whore" pants. The thought had me grinning. I was not a morning person, but damn I needed to find her. She loved my cock, and I had to be a fan of anyone who made that statement.

Maybe a shower first? But my phone was ringing again. It was Chris, our newest, most anxious game designer.

"Ian here," I answered, putting the call on speaker, and heading down the hall toward my kitchen. Orange juice. Coffee. In that order. Did Blessing already have some made? That was where I needed to go first. Maybe see if I could talk her into coming back to bed with me. The monster was up for more fun.

"Ian, what the hell is going on? I heard rumors. Can you confirm?"

I opened the fridge to grab the juice as I said, "If the rumors are that I'm leaving the company, then yes. How did you know?"

"Fucking Josh called me last night trying to talk about a new relationship with the company. Rewrite contracts. I told him I was walking."

"Smart. You don't want to work with that guy."

"I want to work with you. Fucking hell, dude. I saw the clip of the show where they talked about promoting Josh. How the hell did they pass you up and give it to Josh? Did he have naked pictures of your mom or sister or something?"

"My mom? Seriously?" I scoffed, but it did remind me of the conversation I'd had with her recently. This was now my time. I didn't have to do anything I didn't want to do anymore. I could chase my own dream. But what was that now? She would tell me it was best not to make any sudden moves and take time to think things out carefully.

Same thing Blessing said last night.

"No offense, man. Just wondering what the hell is going on. What are you doing? Why did you leave?"

Chuckling, I answered, "I don't want to work with that guy either. He's a fucking moron, but he speaks Harvey's language, so more power to him."

"All right, so you still haven't answered my question. What are you doing now?"

"Still figuring that out. This is all still fresh."

"What the hell…"

"That's pretty much how I felt, too."

"Let's work together, Ian. You were the only guy at the company who knew his shit. You're smart, you've got your fingers on the pulse of the industry, and you know how to do this with your humanity intact. Think about it," he insisted.

This was the second time I'd heard that this morning. My own company. It wasn't something I'd ever considered. "Thanks for all that. I appreciate it. You know VisiStation would take you on in an instant, right. Or another gaming company. I could recommend you."

"I know. But I'd rather hold up a minute and give you a chance to consider. You're my first choice. You could do something epic here. Be

David to their Goliath."

Wow. I grabbed the juice out of the fridge, shut the door, and set it on the counter. Then I rubbed a hand over my face, thinking about the responsibility of it all and what it might entail. "It's a lot to consider, and I haven't even had coffee yet, but I'll let you know what I'm doing in the next day or so."

"All right. I'm not talking out of my ass here. I'm being serious. Talk soon or I'll fucking hound your ass."

I'd just managed to take a swig of my juice before my phone was ringing again. It was going to run out of power soon if I didn't plug it in. Looking down at the screen, my eyes popped wide. James Stephens, the owner of Gamecon, was calling. He was the reason I'd joined the company in the first place. He'd been innovative. Cutting edge. Able to look into the future and see what the next generation was going to be excited about.

"Ian here," I answered.

"Ian, it's Jimmy Stephens. I wondered if you had a minute," he asked, his voice sounding fragile with age.

"Absolutely." I only had the utmost respect for this guy.

"Well, I wouldn't blame you for not taking my call." He sounded rueful. "It's come to my attention that Harvey has made a shit show of my company."

"Yeah, well, he's been the man in charge for

quite some time."

"That's on me." He sighed. "I trusted him to see this company into the future when I decided to retire, but he doesn't have a love for this industry. All he sees is the money."

"I'm sorry to hear that."

"Is it too late to bring you back?"

"I have great respect for you, Mr. Stephens, but there's no way I would ever work for Harvey or Josh."

"I meant bring you back as the President. Hire your own people."

"What about Josh and Harvey?"

He was quiet a moment, likely deciding how he wanted to phrase his words. "There's something shady happening there. We haven't gotten to the bottom of it all yet, but we will. Anyway, there was an emergency board meeting this morning. They have both been fired, and there was discussion about you."

Wow. Go back to the company but leading it? Was that what I wanted to do? It would mean going back to the madness of a job that didn't let me live my life. I'd be back on that treadmill that was always cranked up to a wild sprinting pace. Was that what I wanted? Did I want to go back?

My stomach lurched with a sense of discomfort. It still didn't feel right. At one time, I might have wanted that, but not anymore. Getting off that ride would let me find another that could be exactly what I was always looking for.

But I had to be open for change.

"I'm sorry, Mr. Stephens. I've moved on. I wish you well going forth, but I'll be going my own way."

"I figured. It's hard to keep the good ones. I know that. You've always been loyal to our company and done your best to make it one of the best. Good luck."

"Thanks."

"And if there's anything I can do for you, I hope you'll let me know. Keep my number handy, Ian."

"I will."

My stomach eased. It felt right.
For the first time, I was excited about what the future would bring.

Chapter 17
Blessing

"That's a hickey on your neck!" Layla's exclamation seemed to echo around the boardwalk.

Or maybe it just sounded like that in my mind.

Either way, the heat from the flush bloomed vividly across my face and chest. Could everyone see? I gave a panicked look around the beach front boardwalk but was relieved that we were mostly alone. No one else was out getting breakfast burritos on Sunday at seven in the morning. Layla was the only friend that I knew was an early riser.

Still, I tightened the strings on my hoodie to close the neckline up. I hadn't realized my Hulk had left one.

Instant heat buzzed my pussy, and why, I didn't know. I was not some dopey female that couldn't stand on her own two feet. My eyes found Layla's.

Hers were surprised with a hint of a grin sparkling there. Mine were wide showing the blindside. I had no words. Nothing I could think to say. Even stranger, tears shimmered.

"Blessing! Oh my god. Did he hurt you?" Layla grabbed me in a flash, throwing her arms around my neck. I'd spent the better part of the last three hours working feverishly on the game, again, desperately trying not to remember last night, with no results on either front.

"He would never hurt me," I sniffed as the tears fell. Feeling exposed, I looked around again. No one was paying me any mind. Good thing because they weren't stopping no matter how much I dabbed at them with the sleeve of my hoodie. "Just the opposite."

"Then why are you crying?" she asked, still ready to throw down on my behalf. She was ride or die. I loved that about her.

"It was just too good." Talk about nuts, I even chuckled as tears kept falling. Geez, I was a freak of nature. "I spent the night with him and had amazing sex. He has a magic penis, Layla. I'm experiencing the effects of magic penis syndrome!" I said the last part on a loud whisper, still throwing a look this way and that to make sure no one was listening to me.

"That's wonderful!" she whispered back, taking my cue.

"It's frightening!" I shook my head, still feeling the anxiety I woke up with.

"Why would you be afraid?"

"I don't know if I can do this."

"Why not?"

"Look at me! I'm a mess, and this is after just one night." I swiped the tears from my face while I was laughing. "I'm an independent woman, Layla, but it was like I was clingy and glued to him all night. I can't be that way. He's all I've thought about for days. What the hell is wrong with me? I have gotten nothing done! What the hell am I doing?"

"Doesn't he want a relationship with you?"

"I don't know," I said with some exasperation. "We didn't talk about it. Probably because I left at four in the morning like a dick-whipped ding-bat." More tears were streaming down my face as I laughed. Holy hell, I was going around the bend in grand fashion.

"Four in the morning, Bless? Why would you do that?"

"Well, first, poor Kraken was whining because I didn't take him out to pee after feeding him, so I did that."

"At four in the morning? Isn't that dangerous?"

"He's a Rottweiler," I said, impatient with her interruption. "No one fucks with a hellhound, Layla. Watch *The Omen*."

"Still. Those are movies, not real life. There's a difference." She scowled her disapproval.

"Yes, yes. I'll be careful, mom. Anyway, I came back to the bedroom, and he was lying there all sexy-like with his muscles showing, and the covers shoved down around his waist. I can't even remember how many orgasm he gave me last night!"

"That's fantastic!"

"No! Because then I remembered how he's amazing, taking care of his mother and working his ass off because he needed to do that, but he can never do anything half assed, which means he goes deep and does everything to the best of his abilities, and he succeeds because he is so smart. He commits! Whole-heartedly. And then, the game he created reveals this whole other side that has depth. The world he created, the characters, the themes... He's like me, Layla. He really is just like me, god dammit!"

"Why is this a bad thing? He's a great guy. It sounds like there's potential here. Real potential."

"It is a bad thing because I have it bad for him. Already! Because when I was looking at him this morning, lying in bed all sexy, making me think that I need to wake him for my next magic penis fix, I realized I'm in. All the way in, and I started having a full panic attack."

"I'm still lost, my friend."

"I really, really like him, like him. But it was even more than that. It was like I needed him in this bone deep kind of way. I just want to be around him all the time. Know him. Talk with him. Laugh with him. Fuck him. I'm team Ian, but he might be something else, and why should I let this bother me if I'm a strong independent woman? I've always been proud of being able to do everything by myself, and now I'm freaking out about him!"

"Okay, I think I'm picking up that you're scared."

"Yes! Right? This is so fast. I mean, I met him like a week ago! I'm a rational person, Layla. Rational people don't fall for each other in a week. That would be irresponsible and dangerous. I was having a panic attack about leaving him to go back to my apartment! Can you believe that? So, of course, I had to force myself to just do it. Yank that hot wax strip off my pussy to keep it from prolonging the anguish."

"Hot wax?" Layla shook her head confused.

"Never mind that. It was just, in that moment, I had to leave and stand on my own again and know I could think about something besides him or his beautiful cock and the magic it brings. So yes, I snuck out with my big ass dog at around four in the morning."

"Blessing, sweetheart, he bought the apartment next to yours." She said this gently, kind of rubbing my shoulder like I was feral animal that needed to be calmed. Actually, it was kind of comforting. I swiped at the tears that were still falling and let her pet me.

"Exactly. He's a freaking freak, too, buying real estate before even meeting me. Who does that? Really?"

"Someone who's been thinking about you for a long time. Someone who got the jump on getting to know you because he's friends with one of your good friends and got the full scoop. Was it unusual to buy the property?" she shrugged. "Sure. But he's that kind of guy. Like you said, when he does something, he fully commits. In fact, one could say he was committed to you before he even realized he was committed to you. Hence the move. He'd unconsciously made his decision to get out of this work life. Just my opinion."

I nodded. That did connect up some dots for me. And it was comforting. This thing we were doing…where I actually talked to Layla and let myself be vulnerable, it was okay. It was working out.

"I'm glad I called you, Layla," I sniffed. Swiped at my nose with my sleeve.

"Me, too." She looked at my sleeve. "And that's kind of gross."

"Yeah, I know." I sighed. The leaky faucet behind my eyes finally shut off. "He asked if he could help with the game. He's the friend P-dog said was such a genius. He's the guy Pedro says could probably fix the problem we've been experiencing for the last couple of months in the game."

"So, why not let him help?"

"Because I feel like we should take things slower. I can't just hand it all over. What if I'm wrong? What if this whole thing implodes?"

"You have never risked your heart, have you?" she suddenly realized. Lifting her 'to go' cup of coffee to her lips, she blew on it, watching me over the rim. She took a sip, studying me with a new look on her face.

"What?" I squinted at her. "What's that look? I've dated guys."

"Yeah, but no one ever got under your skin. No one ever blew your mind. No one ever went out of his way for you. No one has ever been so perfect. No one ever made you care."

"Exactly. That right there," I pointed at her. "No one. What if this was a fluke? What if the next time we see each other, he looks at me and is like 'meh' and shrugs. I'm not exactly everyone's cup of tea, Layla. Look at me! I'm short. I'm blind. I live life in a world of fantasy and role play."

"I am looking at you. You are this little package of totally sexy, smart, generous guy fantasy. You have finally found your kind of guy and now you don't know what to do."

"I mean… I know, but…" I didn't know what else to say. I just looked at her helplessly. When have I ever looked at someone helplessly? I was the chick with the answers. I found the solutions. I wasn't the one that ever had the problems.

Oh, shit. Did I have some kind of delusion about what it meant to have problems? Had I just always avoided them before they could even begin? Had I been acting like a coward all this time, and no one had ever called me out on it? I mean, who could? It wasn't like I had a corral of friends.

"Blessing, it's a scary thing," Layla said softly. "When real feelings are involved, there is risk. But if you don't take risks once in a while, you could miss one of the best things ever. When feelings are involved…" she was looking around for inspiration, but I knew what she was trying to say.

"Shit gets real."

"And if you want what you say you want, you have to have courage."

"This is what Bethany was saying yesterday."

"When did you talk to Bethany?" Layla arched her brows with surprise. "I thought you didn't like her."

"When I went looking for you at Zeke's yesterday afternoon. You were busy balling your boyfriend in the office."

The light flicked on in her eyes. A hint of a smile

touched her lips. "Yeah, well, she's a good girl."

"She's all right." I wiped at the excess moisture around my eyes, took my glasses off to clean them before setting them back on my face. "She told me to put my big girl panties on."

"She's right. Be brave, Blessing. You need to be open to the possibilities."

"What should I do? What does that look like?" Fuck, I didn't know how to do this. Be this.

"What do you think need to do to really let him in? To really show trust?"

I needed to be…vulnerable. Just like I'd had to do with Layla. Just like anyone did when it was time to deepen the bonds of a relationship.

We took our separate breakfast burrito bags. I was loaded down because I didn't want to leave my nephews high and dry when they finally came home, and because I wanted to have food for Ian. Each burrito was huge. As soon as I got home, I put one bag in the fridge for whenever the boys were home—even put their names on it. The other, I put on the counter. Wondering if I should go knock or just call through the wall, I compromised and went out on the patio.

He was on the phone when I peeked through his sliding glass door. I held up a foil-wrapped burrito, and he gave me that slow, sexy grin that made my heart beat faster. His eyes roamed over my body as he came to the door and opened it, covering his phone to keep the caller from hearing him.

"You're wearing too many clothes," he purred. "I missed you this morning."

"I bought breakfast," I evaded, wondering how to start a talk with someone. Last night, I was in a flow. That flow was a mixture of anger and guilt and Bethany's pep talk. In the first light of the day, this was all me.

"Let me finish up this call, and I'll be right over."

"I'll get coffee started."

It was just starting to percolate when his hulk form came in through the sliding door. He was wearing his athletic shorts that outlined what I had the pleasure of tasting and feeling inside me last night, and a delicate shiver worked its way up my spine. The memory alone had my pussy starting to pulse again. She remembered. She had a good memory of how amazing it all was.

Magic penis syndrome. It was a thing.

"If you keep looking at me like that, we aren't going to eat for another hour or so at least, and there is a lot to tell you about."

"There is? Did something happen?" I handed him a mug to help himself, opened the cupboard to show him all the fixings. He set the cup down and pulled me in for a deep, all-consuming kiss that scrambled my brain and left me with wet panties. My own hands were up around his neck, grabbing fistfuls of his hair to keep his mouth on mine. More tingles of molten heat swarmed my pussy.

My panties were toast.

I was going to have to change them again.

"Maybe food can wait after all," he murmured, letting his hands roam down my back to grab and squeeze my ass. An involuntary moan escaped my lips.

"But, did something happen?" The words were breathless as I was practically panting from the need he created with a single damn kiss. Talk about scary. I didn't even recognize myself anymore. Was that healthy?

"Jimmy Stephens called to tell me that he wanted me back as President of the company, that he was getting rid of Josh and the current president."

I pulled back. "What? Why? I mean, that's good for them, but why now?"

"All of their top guys are leaving since it got around that I was leaving."

"How did it get around?"

"Josh was calling to renegotiate contracts. Wipe out the opt-out clause I'd put in."

"You put in an opt-out clause?" That was amazing. He truly had been trying to change the company from the roots.

"Yeah. Anyway, none of them want to work with Josh, and the company is now on the brink of losing all of their most valuable assets."

"You were holding the company up."

"I don't know about that," he smirked down at me, but I could see the faint color that rose on his cheeks at my observation.

"Well, I do. And now there's food and coffee. And talk."

"Talk?" His smirk fell instantly, and his voice went dark with a deep, agitated rumble. "What's going on? You are not going to break this off with me. Not after what last night showed us."

"What did it show us?"

"That you're mine. I won't give you up." He was backing me up against the counter, caging me in with his arms.

"Good," I said nervously. "That's good because I've been sitting here thinking of how to go forward with you, and I don't know how to do this."

"What do you mean?"

"I mean, I've never been in a relationship, and I'm used to being on my own. See, I had to learn how to be on my own from the time I was small, so it is the only way I know how to be. I figure things out. I make plans. I execute plans. I help others make plans. You were right about the whole Robin Hood thing. I can do that easily because there's no risk to me."

"That was a bullshit thing for me to say," he interrupted, suddenly grabbing my waist and popping me up to sit on the counter so we were closer to eye level. With his sharp gaze, he held me in place for a beat before continuing with, "I think the way you help others is amazing. Pedro told me about the impact you had in his life."

"Yeah, that might be true, but it wasn't a risk for me to help him." I looked down at my hoodie and thought about the need to wash it. Then I looked back up. "I always tried to be completely self-sufficient, and it got me this far, but it scares me that I'm suddenly so all-in when we only met, like you said, five minutes ago. Shit. I mean, maybe I'm jumping the gun now. What if you aren't all-in, too?"

"What did I say a few minutes ago?" He dipped his head, placing a soft kiss on my lips.

"What?" I kissed him back. "We said a lot of things."

"You are mine." He caught my gaze, wouldn't let me look away. His eyes could just grab me. There was no escape from their intensity. Particularly once he continued: "All parts of you are mine. That includes your problems, your fears, your joys, and your pretty little pussy."

I bit back a moan, still caught in his gaze. My legs squeezed together as another bolt of heat made my pussy clench with desire. If I wasn't careful, it was going to start going down my thighs. When the hell had anyone had that kind of power over me?

"Yes," I said, trying to breathe normally. "But is

the reverse true? If I'm yours, does that make you mine?"

"Absolutely. I'm all yours, little Blast." Now he was eyeing my reaction, his eyes doing their Xray thing through my clothes, like he could see some of the goods. Then he ran his hand down the front of my leggings, sliding his fingers under the waistband of both the spandex and my panties.

I gasped. Opening my legs wider, I asked breathlessly, "Your problems, your fears, your joys, and your giant cock? Mine?"

"All yours. Yes," he growled, and hissed upon feeling the saturation of my pussy folds. He started playing with my slit, letting his fingers dip into the heated center before dragging my slick arousal up toward my swollen clit. "I need to take care of my pussy, baby. She needs me. You keep talking while I take care of business. What else did you want to tell me?"

"While you're doing this?" My voice caught on a gasp as the storm of need grew. My legs shifted farther apart to accommodate his big hand.

"Good girl," he kissed me again. "Is there something you need from me besides an orgasm."

"I don't know how to ask for help."

"Do you need help?"

"I do." I groaned again. "With the game. But I don't want you to feel like you have to help. I mean, only if you want to help."

"I want to be there for you, Blessing. In all things." This his fingers were inside of me, working me, making me cry out as wave after wave of sensation pulsed through my pussy and had me writhing against his fingers. Riding him. When the orgasm hit, I jerked against him. His free arm held me up to his chest while his fingers continued a slow, torturous grind that prolonged the moment. When I came to, I was still breathing hard, and was curled into his embrace. He had his face shoved into my neck.

"You gave me a hickey there last night."

"I know." I felt his grin against my skin. "I did that on purpose."

"Why?"

"Because I wanted to see my mark on you."

"You're an animal."

"Only with you." He placed a languid kiss on the side of my neck and pulled back. "Now, why don't you feed me and tell me about this game issue."

"But what about you?" I let my hand roam over the delicious outline of his athletic shorts where the monster was being sadly neglected, but he caught my hand almost immediately.

"I need to slay dragons for you to earn my reward."

"What is your reward?"

"I need you to wear that costume with the whip."

He stepped back with a wicked look in his

aquamarine eyes. "I might need to tie you up with it."

"I might need to let you do that."

Chapter 18
Ian

It turns out I was the one tied up all night, but just not with my woman.

"You've seen a bit of the game, but now I'm going to show you all of it."

Blessing took a deep, shaky breath, and for a handful of moments, she didn't move. We just stood in the kitchen, and she looked at me through her cute librarian glasses. Wide-eyed. Giving a couple of fluttery blinks.

She was chewing on her lip. Uncertain. A sudden, deep breath seemed to settle her nerves.

It was likely the moment of proof that she was about to trust me.

"Okay. All right," she nodded, mumbling to herself.

"We got this, Blast. We're a team, right? Blast

and Hulk. Let's do this."

"Okay. Yeah." She headed down the hall, and with a feeling like I'd won a major battle, followed her back to the coolest room I had ever been in. She spun her computer chair around and had me sit, facing her three, sleek screens.

"Here is my baby," she smiled, and this time, there was no smirk. There was pride. She went through all of her programs, navigating screen after screen of different worlds, characters, actions. She talked me through how the different worlds were supposed to interlace.

Every piece of it was even more magnificent than I thought it might be. Gorgeous. Perfect. Beautiful. Eerie. Haunting. It covered a range of human emotions and choices. In the midst of the presentation, we got Pedro on a video call, letting him contribute his own information about how he'd gone about trying to fix the glitch.

"You can see that each of the various screens work independently." Blessing showed me while Pedro looked on.

"I just can't make it all work the way it's supposed to. I can't integrate the different worlds," Pedro sighed. "I've been working my ass off. It's crazy. All of the worlds work perfectly on their own, but anytime a character tries to travel between worlds through hidden magic portals, or they try to use their earned rewards to go into the hidden realms, it craps out with an error message."

"I'm okay with coding, not great, so it's no surprise that I can't fix it. But when Spiderman can't fix it, it makes me feel like I'm screwed," Blessing rubbed at her face, dislodging her glasses before pushing them back up her nose. "But he said you're even better at this than he is."

I nodded to show I'd heard them but was still rivetted on the progress of action being projected on all three screens. The realization that this was going to be out in the world soon, that I was going to have a chance to dive into it, was exciting me in a way I hadn't felt in such a long time.

"I appreciate the vote of confidence." I played through the three screens, seeing the attention to detail, hearing the sounds. "Who did the audio?"

"We added that," Pedro was saying. "It's working seamlessly with all of the images."

Blessing seemed to deflate. "And if you can't fix it, I'm totally fucked. In the bad way."

"I'd never let that happen," I murmured, sparing a grin her direction. "We'll get this done."

"This game will get out, one way or the other. It might require us to start from the ground up, rebuild what we're doing one line at a time, but it will get done," Pedro said in what I assumed was supposed to be reassuring.

"That would set us back a few years," Blessing sighed, "but if that's what has to happen, then I guess that's what we do."

"That's worst-case scenario," I told her, still maneuvering through the different screens. "For now, I need to get familiar with what's in front of me. This will not be a quick fix."

"But here's the upside," Pedro called to us through the video call. "If you can figure out the issue, my team and I can jump on it and comb through all code to apply that fix. With all of us working on it, we can get it done in a few weeks at most, as long as it's not catastrophic."

"Then I need to get on this." I took a deep breath. "Give me some time to look through it all. I know you're in a different time zone, so just make sure you answer your phone if I have questions twenty-four hours from now."

"Can do. I'll even be up for a couple more hours here if you need to talk it through."

"All right. Have a good one," I murmured.

"Bye, P-dog! Love you," Blessing blew him a kiss and disconnected the video call. That was the only moment that I turned away from the monitor to deliver a scowl. It was a look she caught.

"What?"

"You love him? Really?" I muttered.

"Of course I do. He's been my friend since childhood." She dropped her hand to my knee and rubbed. "What's going on? Are you jealous?"

"No." I took her hand, raised it to my lips and

kissed her fingers. "Yes."

She giggled. "You don't have to be. He's never been a love interest. Ever."

"Yeah, well, I'm having all these new emotions, so go easy on me." I gave her a pout that brought on her musical laughter. It was my goal. Aside from her sex sounds and the "mad kitten" look, her laughter was another of my favorite things about her.

"What do you need, then?" she asked, coming to sit in my lap. A faint cloud of citrus gently perfumed the air. I had to take a moment and note that it was yet another of my favorite things about her. Nuzzling her neck for a moment, I soaked in the comfort of her warm skin.

One of her hands cupped the back of my head in a comforting caress, playing with the tips of my hair. She was so perfect, but this game was not going to deglitch itself.

This was a job for her personal Hulk to attack.

"I need that burrito you bought me, all warmed up, and a cup of coffee with just some milk in it."

"I can do that."

"Great. Then I can get started right away. Eat while I work."

"Anything else?"

"Yeah." I took a breath and thought about my next sentence. "I would love it if you could take a look at my game and help me improve the artwork.

I've been toying with the idea of updating it."

Her lips parted in a surprised "oh" before a mile-wide smile creased her lips. She quickly said, "I'd love to do that."

"Then we both have a lot of shit to do. I'm going to make a copy of everything before I touch it. I'll upload it to my secure server. Are you okay with that? I've got it protected in ways that might even be illegal."

She smiled. "I trust you."

"I'll always have your back, Blast."

She blinked back a pale blue shine that suddenly appeared, touched by what I said, and nodded. Then she was all business.

And so it happened that hours went by unnoticed. The code was elegant in some places and rough in others. I scanned various worlds. Played through to get a feel for the game, got lost in it, tripped around the gorgeous world Blessing had created, found myself appreciating the whimsy as well as the darker tones, and abruptly got ejected when it came time to seek a treasure in another world.

After experiencing that number of times, I started developing a plan of action. First, I needed to figure out if the two different coding styles were interacting in such a way as to create the dead end. It would be worth it to see if I could create a replacement string of code that would manage the same job without affecting other pieces of code. There was no use fixing one glitch only to create another.

The ideas spun in my head, and I worked through each one systematically, barely aware of Blessing taking care of Kraken, cleaning away our breakfast burritos, and settling herself in with her own sketchpad and art materials.

A persistent ache brought me out of my brain fog, had me arching back to relieve the pain when I realized that the light had changed. The way it was slanting through the windows told me it was getting to be late afternoon, and the moment became so clear to me.

I was working at her computer desk, she was working at her drafting table, and as I suddenly pulled away from the monitor, I just knew that this was exactly how I wanted to spend my life. This was what I'd been reaching for all those years ago.

Blessing had her hair up in a bun with a pencil sticking out of it. At some point, she'd changed into a short denim skirt that had a fringed hem complete with UGGs and an old, threadbare T-shirt that she wasn't wearing a bra under. It was so old, it was practically see-through. Her nipples were pushing up against the thin cotton.

Hmm. When had she put that on?

And was she wearing any panties?

The monster decided it was time to take a break.

We'd skipped lunch without even noticing, until now that is. I was feeling hungry, but not just for food.

I decided to come up behind her, run my hands up her sides and cup her tits. She gasped a moan, lifting her head on an automatic pant as my fingers accurately found her quickly hardening nipples.

"Are you wearing panties, Blast?" I nibbled her neck.

"You should check," she whispered reaching back over her shoulders to grab at my nape, arching her tits straight into my hands.

I let one hand glide up her smooth thigh and up under her skirt only to discover that the dirty little Ms. Sexpot had decided to forgo panties. And she was already wet.

"Did you plan to distract me, Blast?" I asked in a rough whisper, my lips pressed against her lower lobe. Then I nibbled that, too. There wasn't a place on her body that wasn't a feast for my senses.

"Absolutely. Just saving time, Hulk." My cock went rock solid hearing her call me that. Maybe it was my own personal kink, but it worked for me. Then she added, "I was hoping you'd need to put your big cock inside me again real soon."

"I think we can arrange that." Have I mentioned that I love her dirty mouth? Fuck. "Where are the twins?"

"Surfing. They won't be back until dinner."

"That makes things more convenient." I pulled her shirt up to let it rest bunched above her breasts. Her candy pink nipples were already perked up and waiting for my mouth. I was salivating just thinking about them. "You have the prettiest tits, Blast. I love how they taste."

"You want them?" she asked, spinning her seat around.

I bent to put my lips on one and suctioned on, fiercely tonging it, letting my teeth scrape against it. Her breathing was heavy, laced with small, moaning cries of need, especially as I switched to her other nipple. My next move was to pull her off the bar stool and bend her over it. Pulling her skirt up over her ass so her wet little pussy was exposed to me had me groaning my own need.

I couldn't help sliding my fingers through her slick arousal, spreading it around, pinching at her clit so she jerked and cried out until she was begging to have my dick inside her. Then I pulled out my cock and balls over the elastic of my athletic shorts and sank deep into the wet, hot forge of her pussy.

We both groaned, and I had to pause. Grabbing hold of the stool by her hips, I started a slow rhythm that was driving us both crazy, but prolonged the hot, sexiness of it. It wasn't long before I was pounding into her. She brought out the feral Neanderthal in me, until the sound of skin slapping filled the air.

I reached around to play with her clit, surprised to already find her fingers there. Together, we played with her puffy, swollen clit, her fingers directing mine, at the same time that I was pummeling her. Then she was coming hard, squeezing down on my dick until I was hoarsely crying out.

We were still breathing heavily, a fine sheen of sweat on our faces, when I finally pulled out. I let my forehead rest on her back, lifted my face to place a kiss on her nape, rub a hand over her bare ass and help put her skirt back down.

"You have a magic penis."

"Oh yeah?" I smiled as I stood up. "You have an enchanting pussy. I guess that makes us a pair."

"A pair of dorks," she smirked over her shoulder.

So fucking hot. How someone hadn't grabbed her up was beyond me because it was more than just her body that was amazing. It was everything. There wasn't a part of her that I didn't want to completely immerse myself in. She was smart and funny and mine. I was going to make sure of it. She'd lost her chance to be with another guy.

Pulling her around to face me, I planted a rough kiss that echoed my caveman thoughts, but the sound of the dog whining had me breaking it off. "Where's Kraken?"

She looked up at me with a half-smile and a

dazed look. Hearing Kraken's name had her snapping out of it, snapping her head toward the open door. "Oh! He's blocked in the TV room in case we managed to get freaky. You know, nothing kills the mood like have a dog nose in your junk, right?"

"Right," I kissed her again, but this time quick. It was impossible not to. She was so fucking adorable.

"Probably wants food and to go out. Poor baby is crossing his doggy legs and doing his K9 potty dance." She ran her hands over her shirt and skirt.

"By the way," I let my hand run up the back of her skirt again, knead her bare ass. "The no panties thing works for me in a really big way."

"I'll have to remember that."

"I need food. What should we do for dinner? I can cook or we can order something."

"You order whatever sounds good, and I'll take this one out for a walk."

"You're going to put on some clothes first, right?" I didn't like the idea of some douche having the ability to see my delicious playground.

"Yes, Daddy. I promise," she shook her head with a grin.

"I think you said that ironically, but it was actually hot."

Her laughter followed her down the hall. I was following her because there wasn't a time I ever wanted to miss a view like the one she was giving.

Her ass was so perfect. It fit in my hands just right.

She grabbed the leash off a hook by the door and Kraken was there, ready to be taken out, dancing around her feet. Pizza was the easiest thing to order, and I made sure to order plenty. It was a good thing, too, because the guys came home just a few minutes after I'd ordered.

"Blessing, we're home!" one of the twins shouted from the foyer when I was pulling paper plates and napkins out of a drawer in her kitchen. He and his brother had just come in the front door.

"Your aunt's walking the dog, and we have pizza coming."

"She forgave you?" Cody asked.

"Yeah, she did."

"I'm glad. You guys are like rice and sushi. You just go together."

"Rice and sushi?" I arched a brow.

"Or like cheese and pizza." Finn added.

"Fries and burger," Cody insisted.

I laughed. "I think you guys are hungry."

"Starving."

"Food's coming soon."

It was a night of work, and after eating and feeding the twins, I was back at it while Blessing collapsed in bed. The bad news was that it took me most of the night to figure out what turned out to be a complex fix.

The good news was that when I was finished

sharing it with Pedro, I could just walk straight into her bedroom, strip down, curl up around her sexy little body, and anticipate giving her the news.

She was going to be ecstatic.

Chapter 19
Blessing

The news was so devasting, my throat closed up until I could hardly breathe.

"No. Fucking. Way."

It was like the bottom dropped out of this whole project. I felt sick with it. Throwing up was an option with the way my stomach protested what I was reading. Instead, my tears blurred the email sitting in front of me, the one that was breaking my heart so completely.

Thank you for your submission to this year's San Diego Comic-Con International. Due to the overwhelming response by others in your category, we are unable to accommodate all who applied. After careful review of all applications, there were simply a greater number of high caliber projects that we were impressed with. However, if one

should drop out, we can add you to the waitlist.
Please consider applying again next year.

Read it. Reread it. It seemed legit. The email seemed right. The name at the bottom, the Exhibits Director of Operations, was Gina Henderson.

I mean, of course it was right. But the surreal quality of the moment held me suspended in disbelief.

Then the full scope of what she seemed to be saying slapped me in the face in an instant. She'd been less impressed with my work? What the actual fuck? It wasn't of a high enough caliber to be considered worthy of a panel?

Could that be true?

I'd been so sure. The stars had all felt like they were aligned. Everyone had been so enthusiastic in their praise of the art and intertwining storylines. Even Ian. The Shark. He'd come courting me for his big company, not the other way around. Which told me this was high caliber. I'd never really considered I wouldn't get in.

But I'd worked so hard.

For so long.

Tears spilled down my cheeks as the gargantuan mountain of worry, stress, excitement, and utter exhaustion that had accumulated over the years of my life that I'd dedicated to this singular project, crashed right on top of me. Consumed me. Drops splashed hot and wet onto the front pockets of my hoodie, and with that rush of emotions, it was like I could only take gasping breaths of air through the tightening bands around my chest.

What was I going to do now?

"Shit," I whispered on an exhale as more tears flooded my face. Two days in a row. So damned emotional. Was I about to start my period? If I wasn't careful, I'd end up on a reality show.

My self-directed humor wasn't helping. If I didn't get ahold of myself, I was going to hyperventilate. But I couldn't seem to stop myself. I was just so tired. I'd been paddling so long and so hard up this river, and it had all led to nothing.

I'd been counting on this. Dammit!

I hadn't made other plans.

Fighting back more tears, I took a deep breath. Swiped at my eyes and kept sniffling. It was hard to calm myself. It was like the floodgates had opened, but at least I was breathing regularly again.

There were other ways. I knew there were. I just hadn't thought of them yet. But I could be forgiven for needing a minute to be disappointed. To cry. Of course, this rejection had always been a possibility, but I hadn't let myself sit in that place. I'd been hyper-focused on envisioning success, but this was a lesson. You couldn't take anything for granted.

And yet, how many things had I taken for granted? Poo-pooing the idea of a gaming company courting me because I was too good for that. Who did I think I was? So goddamn superior. Always coming down from Mt. Olympus, but here was my comeuppance, right? It was like Ian said, playing Robin Hood when it was easy, when I wasn't having to sacrifice anything, was a luxury. Ian, who'd spent years putting himself on the back burner. And I was questioning his integrity.

God, I was a bitch.

And what was Ian doing now?

Ian was crashed out on my bed because he'd spent the night working to help me, and I'd been pushing him away? Had I even thanked him? I couldn't even remember if I had. Was I taking him for granted too?

With hardly a thought, I left the office, Kraken my ever-present, loyal minion, followed me back upstairs to his big doggie bed. I left him there with a scratch behind his ear before continuing back to my bedroom where I could stare down at Ian's big, masculine form sleeping in my fluffy, feminine comforter. His large form was sprawled chest down across two-thirds of the space, his face relaxed on my pillow instead of his own. All it took was seeing him there to rev my sex engine, get the lube flowing.

Fuck, he was hot.

My Hulk.

He rushed into danger to save me from a potentially real Kraken.

He'd worked all night on my game design without question.

He'd moved his whole life to be here with me. How amazing was that? How often did an amazing man do that for a woman?

I must have made some noise because his beautiful eyes blinked open, a sleepy smirk barely touched his lips upon seeing me, but it faded the longer he looked at me, concern furrowing his brows. "Blessing?"

In response, I shucked my sweatpants and pulled my hoodie off. He sat up slowly, first appreciating my body, then studying my face as I climbed on the bed and straddled him. He wrapped his arms around me to pull me tight to his big, warm chest. Being skin-to-skin felt so intimate, so close. He held me tight, his face finding the crook of my neck and inhaling deeply, like he was finding comfort in me. I had never been someone's source of comfort before.

My arms snaked around his shoulders, loving the silky texture of his dark hair threaded around my fingers, and I inhaled a comforting breath of him right back.

"What's the matter, baby," he asked in his low rumble, worried.

I kissed his neck behind his ear, fighting the tears again. He was really so kind. I mean, I'd known that about him. He'd fucking taken care of his mother.

Put his life on hold for her. Was he doing that for me, too?

"Blessing?" he pulled back to look at my face when I didn't respond immediately. I hadn't been so successful in keeping my tears hidden. He reached a hand up to wipe the wetness from my cheeks. "You're killing me, sweetheart. What happened?"

"How long were you up last night?" I asked instead, biting my lip to keep it from quivering.

He suddenly smiled big. "Not going to lie. It was late but let me tell you the good news. I figured out a fix. I swear, I experimented on the code so many fucking ways, and it wouldn't work, or would cause another chain reaction glitch, but then I hit on it. I think. I'm pretty positive. I sent the fix to Pedro, so his team could have some fun with it. Bottom line? We're on the last lap of this race, baby Blast. But it was a good time. I forgot how much I love creating code and solving problems."

Even through my tears, my grin matched his, his excitement burst through my bubble of pity, and I squeezed him tight, thinking there was no way I would ever let this man go again. He was mine. My sex engine revved hotter. Wetter.

I felt the monster responding beneath me under the covers at Ian's waist and pulled back with an arched brow.

"You're sitting on my dick, Blast. And you're naked. And you're the sexiest fucking woman in the world. It's going to happen."

The sexiest. He'd said that. Tears didn't spill, but they shimmered as my eyes caressed his face.

I sat up to get the covers out from under me, give my pussy a chance to feel his velvet steel against my slick folds. His long, deep groan was the best music, and my hips moved to it. My pussy slid along his hot, growing length with a deliberate stroke, holding his beautiful gaze, steadily, wanting to show him the feelings that were deep inside of me.

"Thank you," I whispered, moving my hips again causing a delicious, tingling blood rush between my thighs that had me sucking in a breath at the exquisite feel of us. Together.

In the grand scheme of things, today's problem was a setback. It wasn't world-ending. What was most crucial in this moment was letting this man know how important he'd become to me. I wanted to be worthy of him.

"You didn't have to help me," I breathed out shakily, rocking my wet slit along his shaft.

I wanted to keep him. In my life. In my bed. In my heart and mind. I'd never thought I could do that before, and I couldn't with anyone else. But I could. With him.

A heavy surge of slick heat flooded my pussy and coated his cock, and I picked up my movements. Moved my hips a little faster. His breath caught, and his eyes grew heavy, but he didn't look away. He seemed to feel the difference, know that this was more. I wanted more than a quick fuck. I wanted more than an exchange of quips. I wanted more of him. All of him.

"It was my pleasure," he breathed heavily, his eyes staying with me, even as his hands slid up my ribcage to cup my breasts, play with my nipples. That was all it took to have me moaning with the ever-growing pleasure that wracked my body.

"It means so much to me," I managed, but it wasn't the only thing I wanted to say. Gathering courage, I said, "You mean so much to me, and I'm so glad we met."

"You're mine, Blast," he said gruffly. "All of you."

I raised up to guide his cock into my heat and did a gentle slide down onto his hard length. Pausing to savor the feel of him hot and pulsing inside of me, stretching me, I cupped his precious face and kissed him gently, shaping and contouring his firm, soft lips with nibbling bites and gentle sucking. My hips rocked against him. As the intensity grew, we were moaning gasps against each other's lips, pulling back to watch the pleasure build on each other's faces.

Then, in a smooth roll, Ian had me under him, his body on mine, a welcome weight that was settled between my legs. Sliding into me again, his big, rough hand caressed a path down my side, around my hip, and jacked my leg up for leverage to go deeper.

Each thrust was hard and sharp. With each movement of his hips, he grunted his driving need, and I cried out with the pleasure that was becoming almost too much.

"Ian," I whimpered as he increased his pace, pistoning his hips until my orgasm hit me full force and my inner walls clamped on to him, milked him fiercely, just as he snarled his own release.

I clung to him, shaking, just wanting to feel him, be as near to him as I could. He was a touchstone I didn't know I needed, and it seemed I was that for him as well. He rolled over, pulled me on top of him to keep from crushing me, but his hands kept moving over me in the gentlest of touches. Smoothing hair off my face, running a hand down over my back to my ass.

"I don't know what's going on with us," I whispered near his ear, "but I know that I want what's happening. I want to be an us."

"It's a good place to start," he murmured, "but know that I'm going to be pushing for more. My need to be around you is becoming an addiction."

I huffed a laugh and snuggled closer.

"So what was going on earlier? What's happened?"

I sighed. "Gina Henderson sent me an email

from Comic Con letting me know that my application has been rejected."

"I didn't realize you were waiting for them to get back to you."

"I've been waiting on pins and needles." I shook my head but continued. "What bothered me was that I realized I wanted to be someone worthy of you."

"What does that mean?"

"It means that I've never had to face adversity, and you've only faced it."

"Don't do that, baby. Don't compare. We've all been dealt our own hand of cards by the universe. It's what you do with that hand that matters."

"But you were right that I haven't had it hard. I've had it pretty easy. There hasn't been a real struggle for me, but you've had to struggle forever.

"Blessing, you could have spent your time having fun and turning a blind eye to the people around you. Instead, you helped people. Pedro. Layla. Me. You aren't afraid to jump right in because of who you are. You're one of those people who's aware that you've had it good, so you want to make sure you help others build their confidence, so they can find their own place in the world. You transform people. They become better for having met you. Just like in your game."

The mention of the game had tears coming to my eyes again. "I'll be okay, really, but I was sure I had this one in the bag. There are probably a thousand ways I haven't thought of to accomplish the same goal. It'll just take time."

It was Ian's turn to scowl.

"What?"

"What did you say the name was on the email?"

"Gina Henderson."

"It can't be coincidence. And, it's fucking Sunday. No one sends business email on a Sunday." Ian suddenly rolled out of bed and pulled his sweatpants up. When he disappeared into the computer room, I got up and dressed quickly to follow him.

"What?" I asked, coming up behind him, yanking my own sweats back on.

"That name. Josh's last name was Henderson. I don't believe in coincidence. I'm wondering if he has a family member working for the convention."

"No way. Would he really do that?" I thought of his shady smile and dickish attitude and reached my own answer at the same time Ian confirmed it.

"In a heartbeat." He'd left his phone charging on my desk. He grabbed it up. "I'm going to call Sal to see if he knows anything about Josh's extended family."

But just as he was about to start dialing, his phone rang. It was Josh.

"Ian here," he said as he put it on speaker.

"Did you like my parting gift?" Josh asked,

sneering vindictively. I could imagine that evil glee radiating from his stupid face the way it had when I first met him.

"What gift was that?" Ian asked.

"Maybe you haven't look at emails yet. It's Sunday after all, and yet, I find myself having to look for a new job."

"Good. Maybe one outside of this industry since you don't know shit about it. Why the fuck Harvey ever hired you—"

"Oh, he didn't have a choice." He laughed, a barking sound that was lacking in real humor. "I knew about his girlfriend and threatened to tell his wife."

"Now it all makes sense," Ian muttered, shaking his head.

"What did you do?" I asked, stepping closer to Ian. "What is your parting gift?"

"Hey there, Blessing. Well, my stepsister is on the Comic Con selection committee. She is always happy to help her little brother get even with his enemies. I figured you were working that angle, and low and behold, your application was right there."

"You had her reject my work? Are you serious?"

"Thank your boyfriend. It's his fault that I'm out of a job."

"You are one stupid sonofabitch, you know that? You're out of a job because you're inept. Let me tell you how inept you are, Josh. My connections within that organization and within this industry are strong. You just fucked over your stepsister."

"What do you mean?" he snarled.

"You didn't think this through, did you? Do you want to warn her to start looking for a new job, too, or do you just want her to be surprised? I'm also going to enjoy scheduling an exclusive interview detailing how Gamecon completed a final death spiral the moment you were in charge. Do you think any media outlets will be interested in that story? You'll never work in this industry again."

"You can't do that." He was starting to sound panicked.

"Go fuck yourself, Josh, and don't call here anymore."

"You can't do that," he shouted again, his angry voice radiating from the phone. "This isn't over yet!"

"Cue the evil laugh track again," I smirked over at Ian. "Just hang up on him. He's a loser with the losingest loser attitude in Loserville history."

"Whatever you say, my Blast." His smile was warm and tender, aimed at me, as he terminated the call. "I've always got your back. Which brings me to my next question: Want to form a company with me? I've been thinking about that because a few of my old clients have been messaging me. It could be you, me, and Pedro's company. We could help manage some of the designers, and we could work on our own games besides. Best of both worlds."

"Wow. Really? Wow." I took a deep breath and realized it was a new day. Exhilaration flooded my system, and I had to throw myself into his arms again. He caught me, because he's the Hulk of course, and laughed.

"I take it that's a yes?"

"I've had that on my mind for a while now. I mean, that would be great." I pulled back to look up at him, feeling like all the hearts and flowers were shining from my eyes. "What would we call it?"

"I've thought about that, too." There was a definite twinkle in his aquamarines when he paused for effect. I waited with bated breath for a solid beat before he finally said, "We could call our gaming company 'Glitch.'"

My excited grin was both instant and a mile wide.

"Perfect!"

Chapter 20
Ian

Early mornings were the best time to get my ass handed to me by a wave, was my takeaway from the last few days.

I'd been coming out to the beach at the first light of dawn since the twins went home because it was a quieter time of day. There were fewer people out in the water, fewer surfers to share the waves with.

It was where I regularly ran into Mason.

I surged up from under the whitewash, swiping water out of my eyes, to the sound of him hooting his laughter. Couldn't blame him; that'd been a good one. I'd dropped into the wave too hard, too fast, and lost my balance. From there, I'd taken a header straight to the board. The movement of the wave had suddenly thrust it up into my face and thwacked me across the side of my forehead. The force of the water tossed and tumbled me like I was a rag doll. I snorted water and scraped a rock; though, I was lucky enough to be wearing a thick wetsuit or else it would have torn the shit out of my skin.

If nothing else, the ocean taught humility.

"Thought I was going to have to save your ass," Mason taunted, a wide grin creasing his face. "I was sure you were knocked the fuck out."

"Almost was," I responded as I paddled back to where he was bobbing on the waves. Feeling noodled, I tried to ignore the feel of muscle burn in my arms and shoulders from paddling almost nonstop the last hour and a half. "This shit is hard."

"But it keeps you honest." Mason held out his knuckles for a fist bump after I sat on my own board.

I reached out my fist for a quick tap, a self-deprecating shake of my head. "That it does."

"It'll come easier over time. Been doing this for years. It only gets better."

"I could see that happening," I replied, looking out over the horizon where the endless expanse of blue-gray water kissed the sky. It had been a couple of days since Blessing had received the news about San Diego, and I'd practically been living at her place. "It looks like I'll be staying around."

"I heard about the San Diego thing. Is everything going to go okay for Blessing?"

"I'm working on that," I scowled, looking back toward shore as though I could somehow see her. Remembering her tears from the other morning still had the power to piss me off. Made me want to slay all of her dragons, spill blood in retribution. "I've been to Comic Con every year. I've made important connections. Hell, *I* am an important connection. The right person will answer for this. The pain will be delivered swiftly. I promise you."

"That's what I'm talking about." Mason's grin had an evil appreciation to it. "She didn't deserve to be fucked over. By anyone." He was looking at me meaningfully.

"I'm not going to fuck her over."

"Do you love her?"

That caught me off-guard. I needed a moment to sit and stare at him. Think about it. Feel the truth of how I was feeling.

"That's a big question." My heart pounded. Did I love her? She was quickly becoming embedded in my DNA. Was that love? I couldn't imagine not being with her. That was how quickly we became coded together. Intertwined. Complete only when integrated. "I've never felt this way about another person. I think we're both still working through our feelings."

"That's fair," Mason nodded. "Sometimes it's hard to see what's right in front of you, but when you meet someone who's got your back, magic starts to happen. Seriously. It's one of the beautiful things we get to be part of. Meeting Layla saved me. I'd just say to you, be open to it. Let it happen."

"Yeah, well, we definitely have some kind of magic happening." I sat on the water, floating on the power of the ocean, and appreciating that I had no control over anything. There was comfort in that. My mom had been sick and now she was healthy, and maybe she would get sick again, but there was nothing I could do about that. The anxiety was lessening with my time here.

Control what you could control and let the chips fall where they may. And back home, I had a sexy, sweet, fierce, genius, force of nature, who was sound asleep in bed, naked. Maybe I could get back there before she got up. That, I could control.

"So tell me what's in her computer room. She's never let anyone else in there," Mason cocked a brow.

"It's top secret, amazing shit." I gave him a grave look. "I could tell you, but then I'd have to kill you."

He chuckled, shook his head.

"But seriously, you'll find out before too long. This is going to be huge."

"I'm looking forward to it."

It wasn't long after that we both paddled in, ready to collapse. Mason didn't live far. With a quick grunt and casual salute, he grabbed his board and went off to find breakfast and drive his woman to work.

Just as I was about to grab my small, cloth backpack and board and start the walk back to the apartment, my phone rang. Fishing it out, I saw that it was my old CEO, Rick Montoya, and I remembered that I hadn't called him back. He'd called a few days ago.

"Ian here," I picked up.

"Ian! I'm glad I finally caught you."

"How are you doing, Rick?" I was half afraid to ask the question, thinking he'd reply that he had some kind of terminal illness. "How are you feeling?"

"You know, you're the only one who sent flowers to the house the last few months. I never expected that, and I wanted to thank you."

"Uh...you're welcome. I mean, it wasn't any big deal. I just remember what my mom went through when she was in the hospital. Flowers kept her spirits up. I don't know what you're going through, but I hope you're going to be all right."

"Well, to tell the truth, I'm feeling like a million bucks. A good job will do that for you."

"A good job?" I stared out at the rolling waves, confused. "What are you talking about?"

"I was never sick, Ian. It's what I implied, but actually, I've changed gears. I'm working with a production company. We're making movies, Ian.

It's cutting-edge stuff."

"That's cool, man. First, I'm glad to know you're healthy, and second, congratulations. Couldn't have happened to a better guy. You earned this after working for Harvey."

"Yeah, about that. I heard there was a lot of shit going down with Gamecon. Harvey and his little lap dog were such fucking pricks."

"Yeah, well they are officially unemployed." I looked down at my phone. It was getting later, and I wanted to get home before Blast woke up. Waking her up was fun. The confused look on her face as she ground her pussy against my mouth, still blinking sleep from her eyes, was a thing I didn't want to miss. Of course, I could always enjoy unwrapping her again if she was already dressed.

"Hasta la vista, right?" Rick was saying.

"What's going on, Rick?" I asked, wanting him to come to the point of his call. "I don't understand. If you weren't sick—"

"The place was killing me, Ian. It was sucking me dry. It was taking away my humanity, my joy, my creativity, and turning me into something I told myself I would never become."

I nodded, encouraging him with a quick, "I know what you mean."

"I'm sure you do. When I hired you, I knew you were going to be good for the company, and you were. It's only because of you that I could afford to make the move I did."

"What move is that?"

"I'm with Follow the White Bunny Studios. I know you've heard of them."

I had. My eyes grew wide as I stared out at the waves. "Holy shit, Rick. That's epic. They are cutting edge. Up and coming. What they've done so far has been ground-breaking. You've landed a fucking great job, not just a good job."

"And here's where you come in."

"Me?"

"Let me ask you, what are you doing now that you no longer have to kiss the ring. Not that you ever did. I enjoyed the many varied ways you told Harvey to fuck off without actually telling him to fuck off. Opt-out clauses? Genius. They did themselves in. There's poetry in that."

"Well, I've got a tentative plan to put my own company together. I'm working with some amazing people on that, and I've got a handful of game designers that want to join the team."

"Perfect. What I'm about to tell you is confidential, but I trust you. I always have."

"I appreciate that."

"So, listen up. Tech is making a big splash these days. Everyone loves to see their favorite gaming characters come to life on film, so we're doing a fun, family-friendly movie where a kid manages to tear a hole in the fabric of the universe. At this point, a variety of gaming characters come to life from different games. There will be epic battles from different worlds, and the kid has to help defeat the most evil of the characters who have all banded together to fight the good guys."

"What do you need from me?"

"I need a major game recommendation, something that will bring it all together. Something new. Something we haven't seen before."

"The movie sounds like a morality play." The stars were aligning, as Blessing would say. My heart kicked up as I realized this was exactly the right introduction for *Multiverse: Infinity.*

"It is. We're hoping to release it a year from now. Next Christmas. We already have big names attached to the project, and live-action filming starts after the holidays."

"Rick, I'm so glad you called me. I have found a game so big and beautiful, that's it's almost too big for the small screen. I would love to show you."

"I knew it. I knew you would have something for me. You're the fucking Shark. Let's get you on the calendar. When can you show us what you've got?"

"I'm pretty sure later this week will work for us. I'll need to check in with my partners on this."

"I'll have my assistant call to set something up. We'll need to get things underway. There's going to be a time crunch on this. By the way, you have a company name?"

"Yeah. As soon as we make it all legal, it's going to be Glitch."

"Catchy. I like it. You still have Sal working for you?"

"Not yet, but I'll get him before Gamecon totally collapses."

"Soon, Ian. I mean it. This week. We need to get this ball rolling. Time is money."

"Absolutely."

I made it back to the apartment in record time. Blessing was going to freak the fuck out, and I couldn't wait to see it happen. Dumping my board and wetsuit out on the patio, I sailed through the sliders on Blessings side before coming to a mad halt.

I couldn't believe who she was sitting with.

Chapter 21
Blessing

How do you think I looked when I answered the door?

Well, considering it was like we'd lifted the lid off Pandora's sex box, it was no surprise that chaos ensued; we went at it like monkeys all night. My pussy deserved a medal for valor while under heavy fire, but, of course, the naturally occurring rewards were more than sufficient. Highly desired. Greatly appreciated.

The orgasms had not only been plentiful, but mind-blowing. I needed to make a sign and hang it over the bed. I was incorporating it into my new belief system: *To find true happiness, orgasms must be plentiful and mind-blowing.*

It might have to become a thing.

Which brought me back to the present. We'd

fucked all night, and I looked like it. Probably smelled like it, too. With the way we'd been working and fucking almost nonstop, I knew I needed a shower. So why did I answer the knock at the door wearing only a threadbare T-shirt that barely covered my ass? Because I thought it was Ian. I thought he forgot his key and needed to be let back in.

Yes, I gave him a key. Why? Because at this point, the idea of being apart for even a night, even when he was living next door, made my stomach ache. Literally. It gave me indigestion. I'm not even kidding. And how was that even possible? In the space of a single week, I went from being a hermit, or near to, to wanting Ian so much that I was sick with it.

That made me clingy, didn't it?

That had to be a problem. There was probably a support group for people like me.

And, of course, it wasn't Ian at the door.

It was his mom.

His freaking *mom* was standing there, fighting back chuckles at the sight of me.

I knew it was her—I saw the resemblance immediately with her tropical blue-green eyes and long dark hair, though she was sporting an impressive sweep of silver in the lock that fell over her forehead.

She was adorable in her mom jeans and blue

sweater that had dolphins on it.

"You're Ian's mother, aren't you?" I cringed inwardly.

The full reality of the situation hit me. I knew I looked like a hundred miles of bad road as I gave a quick glance down at my clothing, and involuntarily reached out a hand to push up my glasses and smooth down the "just fucked" look of my hair. Was I sporting racoon eyes, too? I didn't even want to look because to see was to know.

"I am. Please call me Edie," she said showing off dimples in both cheeks. "And you're the girl he's talked about? Who lives next door to him? There's no one else who lives in the building, am I right?"

He talked about me? To his *mom*? And now she was *here*? And he didn't *warn* me? Two simultaneous feelings occurred: one was more along the lines of "What the fuck, Ian" while the other was more of a heartfelt "Ohhh…" with warm fuzzies attached.

I was so out of my element. My heart stumbled a few times, beating erratically as the nervous energy swept over me. There had never been a time when I'd met someone's parent. What was I supposed to do?

Maybe not keep her out in the hallway. Maybe offer a place to sit and be comfortable. Sheesh, Batman. Get a grip. Since when had I become socially inept? Maybe since I was going to flash my pussy if I bent over.

Fuck.

"I'm that girl," I admitted with a quick tilt of my lips.

In the next instant, she was hugging me tightly.

"Oh!" I gasped, not expecting it but hugged her back. It was a general policy to warmly welcome a boyfriend's mother into the home, right? Not that I would know, never before having had one.

Shit, I had a boyfriend. Just the word was foreign on my tongue. So new and different. Connection. A unit. A team. Boyfriend. Wow. But that's what he was, right?

Or was he? We hadn't actually said that out loud.

"You are a blessing," she pulled back, and I swear her eyes were misty. Pink, even.

"Umm...Yes. That's my name."

"Your name? Is 'Blessing'?" Then her head tilted back, and she laughed. "Of course, it is. Because my son needs the universe to literally spell it out for him. He needs the universe to smack him upside his head to recognize what's right in front of him."

"Oh," I said again for the second time in two minutes. That was so sweet. My own eyes burned. "Thank you for that, but I'm the lucky one. I'm so glad he decided to be stalkerish and buy the place next door before he even met me."

"He did that?" she gasped. A second peal of

laughter came from her lips. "Of course he did. He gets so focused, and he doesn't stop until he gets what he wants. Very singular attention span, even when he was a kid."

"Please, come in, Edie. He's out surfing right now and should be back soon, but I have some coffee we can make." I moved out of the way to make room for her to enter. "I have a very comfortable couch where we can sit and enjoy a view of the cloudy marine layer that we get every morning, and we can get to know each other."

"That sounds wonderful," she clapped her hands together and rubbed them as though to ward off the chill. She walked straight toward the back of the place where the glass doors gave a view of the ocean. "It's surprisingly cold out here. I know it sounds silly, but I thought it would be warm because it's the beach."

"A lot of people make that mistake," I assured her, coming up next to her. "Especially if they don't spend a lot of time here. I can get you a sweater or a jacket."

"I'm fine. Truly." She faced me suddenly, studying me for a beat of silence before reaching out to take both of my hands in her own. "I trust Ian one hundred percent in the choices he's made. They haven't always been easy, and I'm sorry for that. It was rough there for a while, and his focus became all about taking care of me when I was sick."

"He told me you survived cancer."

"Breast cancer. Those were dark times, and everything he did was for me. Because he's fierce about taking care of the people he loves. Even if it means burying his own dreams."

"He's a beautiful person," I whisper. "I just want to be worthy of him. He does so much for without even being asked."

"The fact that he picked you says you are, in my mind. And I wanted to come celebrate this with him. Finding you. There was something new in his voice when he spoke to me about you. It made my heart sing to know that he was finally going to get what he's always wanted. He was going to be happy, not just because I was in remission, but for himself."

"I think he's trying to do that now."

"And that's why when he mentioned you, how he'd moved here suddenly, I knew I had to meet you. Get to know you." She pulled me in for another tight hug, adding, "We're going to become good friends, you and I. That I can promise."

I held her tight, knowing he was from her, that she was of him, and that she was so important that he sacrificed aspects of his life to make sure she got the care she needed. "Okay, you are officially going to make me cry."

"Don't cry, sweetheart. But I would recommend getting some clothes on before you bend over too far, and I get to know you too personally. Point me in the right direction, and I'll get the coffee going while you get changed."

I pulled away with a laugh. "Now I want to flash you just for the hell of it."

"We will definitely be friends."

And that was how I ended up back in my leggings and hoodie. My hair was tossed up in a loose bun, a mug of coffee in hand, and shooting the breeze on my sofa with Edie Patrick when Ian appeared.

I saw him enter into the patio area and had to catch my breath. He was so big. So vibrant. Larger than life. My heart sped up at the sight of him. My eyes feasted, cataloging every movement of his body. After dumping his board and wetsuit outside, he came through the glass doors wearing a sweatshirt, boardshorts, and flipflops, and stopped dead in his tracks.

"Mom!" he grinned, coming in. It was adorable to see his tough, manly features turn boyish.

"Ian," she greeted, with warmth and love overflowing her words.

Edie stood up from the couch, and he swooped in to give her a tight hug. He was a great hugger, and all it took was meeting her to know that he learned it from his mom. Hugs were important. Feeling like someone had a hold of you, like you were important, was the best feeling.

She pulled back and reached up to cup his scruffy jaw. "I'm so glad to see you."

"What are you doing here?" He suddenly frowned. "I was going to come visit soon. You shouldn't be driving this far. It's dangerous."

"I'm not a child, Ian. I can drive myself now," she said with some exasperation. Then she was back to grasping one of his hands between her own. "Besides, I needed to see for myself. I wanted to look in your eyes and see it."

"See what?"

"Your smile. Your happiness."

"Well, I just made the deal of a lifetime, so I should definitely look happy. I was just coming in to tell Blessing about it." He glanced over at me, and in a fraction of a second, he gave me a look that told me he liked what he was seeing, and that was when I realized we could actually become one of those couples. The kind that can communicate with meaningful looks and overly long stares.

"No, no." Edie shook her head, not letting him get away with a trivial response. "I haven't seen you truly happy in a long time. I haven't seen one of your real smiles since before I got sick, and I had to come and see it for myself. We've been there for each other, sweetheart, and there was no way I was going to miss out on seeing you follow your heart."

"I am happy, Mom. You're right. It's been a while, but I wouldn't change anything."

"I know you wouldn't. Things happen as they should. And now it's time for you to find your own adventures."

He pulled her back into a hug and rested his chin on top her head, meeting my own eyes across the room. The commitment was there in his steady, piercing gaze when he said, "I promise. And a big reason for why is because Blessing inspires me."

"Me?" My brows shot up. My cheeks flushed with pleasure, even as I said, "No way. I mean, maybe a little, but you were ready. It was time."

Edie pulled away again. "It was definitely time. I love you, sweetheart, and I can't wait to see what's next."

"I love you, too, Mom. And as to what's next..." His eyes held a gleam of excitement, and I knew he had something to tell me. See? We were becoming one of those telepathic couples. That alone was going to make me cry.

"What's up, Hulk?" I asked, covering my newly found sensitivity with a smile.

"Well, Blast, I just had an interesting conversation with Follow the White Bunny Studios. They need a fresh, epic game that no one has seen before to be featured along with other iconic game characters in a new movie they have coming out a year from now. We have a meeting to set up this week to show them what we've got because they needed to get rolling on this yesterday."

"What?" I was having trouble understanding what he'd just said.

"The premise of this thing is the characters. Some kind of tear-in-the-universe thing where a kid accidentally starts a superhero war with all new superheroes and villains. It could be huge. You know how people love the big-effect CGI crossover between the animation and the real?"

"Holy shit." My hand covered my mouth, trembling. "My game? *Multiverse Infinity*?"

"Your game is potentially going to be known around the world. And yes, we will be going to Comic Con. The studio has a panel to talk about this new movie that will bring gamers out of the woodworks, and we'll be there for promotion. Big promotion. Showstopping promotion. Studios usually pull out all the stops. I've seen how this gets done."

This was even more than I could have hoped for. It was everything. How had all of this happened?

"If they like it, right? I mean, they could still veto it." It was hard not to have some doubts creep inside the joyful bubble, even as I felt the flutters of excitement in my gut.

"Oh, trust me. They will. They want a meeting with us ASAP. We need to pull our collective shit together, get Pedro on board, and storm the goddamn castle. Batman, Hulk, and Spiderman. Do you get what I'm saying? This is it. You have arrived."

And I somehow knew he was going to be right.

"Oh my god!" I shouted, bouncing up from the couch to beeline for Ian, throwing my arms around both him and Edie in my excitement. "We did it?! We did it!! And we can go as Sage and Storm from the game. And maybe we can get friends to go as different characters."

Edie joyfully participated in our excited group hug. "I get this is a big thing. You guys have to tell me about it."

"How long can you stay?" I laughed, bouncing on my toes.

"It's still early morning," Ian stepped back. "Let me get changed and take my two best girls out for some breakfast. We can talk more then."

Chapter 22
Blessing

I checked myself in the mirror and knew I looked perfect.

It was an authentic costume, attention drawn to the most intricate detail. The golden-plated, writhing-snake arm and wrist bands wound around my limbs in their rightful place. The gold-plated metal collar was around my neck with a length of chain hanging down my back. I'd been saving this Princess Leia bikini costume for a special occasion, and I couldn't think of a better time.

I even had my hair braided, laying between my gold-encased breasts.

It had been a few weeks since his mother, Edie's, first visit, but now she was back with a couple of her friends for the holidays. We'd spent the day decorating our Christmas tree and putting up lights around the room. I'd insisted on baking sugar cookies and decorating them because wasn't that what all happy couples did in the Christmas movies?

And there were so many colorfully wrapped gifts under the tree. What they represented is what made my eyes shimmer. It was like I was actually starting to have my own little family, right here. I was becoming a full on grown up. In the good way. There was even something wrapped for Kraken.

Yes. We were keeping him.

Our newest family member, Kraken, had to be kept away from the tree, so he wouldn't consider it his personal pee spot. In the last few weeks, he'd received his shots along with a clean bill of health. He'd also moved his bed to a corner of our bedroom, not wanting to be left out of the pack when it was time for sleep. Grabbed the big cushion with his teeth and walked it down the hall.

Ian drew a line against letting him sleep on the bed. We still found him there at times. It was cute. He tried to be sneaky, like a hundred-twenty-pound dog could be sneaky in any way.

We'd also fallen into our new habits, which included always having a shadow and never getting to pee alone again. Kraken was insistent on sitting next to me while I was on the potty, because if not, he'd whine outside the closed door. It sounded so sad, I didn't fight it.

Pathetic. Me, not him. He was absolutely my newest, bestest friend who listened attentively to all of my best and worst bits of stream of consciousness with equal amounts of high alert attention.

Christmas Eve was two days away, and the plan was to cook with Ian's mother with some early gift giving. She was also going to meet my family. They were beyond excited to finally meet who I was bringing home. My parents were going to host a big meal as per usual on Christmas Day while we watched some football and opened gifts, something Layla was a part of, which was always fun. Now Mason would be with us, and I couldn't wait to bring Ian around. We were all going to get along like a house on fire.

That was a good thing, right? Whatever.

My parents would be thrilled that I was finally bringing someone home that I was in love with, and that was part of what was going to make tonight special.

The biggest new? I was going to tell Ian I loved him. Tonight.

"Hey Kraken. Good boy." I heard Ian's deep, rumbly voice coming through the slider. There were whines of excitement as the puppy got his demand for attention met.

I grabbed my terrycloth robe and pulled it tightly over the bikini top, making sure that the burgundy material hanging from the gold-plated medallion belt around my hips wasn't showing below the hem of the robe in the front or the back. I'd made a modification only in that I wasn't wearing actual bikini bottoms. Only the material was shielding my pussy. But I wasn't ready for him to see it yet.

"Blast! Where are you?" he called out.

I grinned, anticipating his reaction to my outfit.

"I was just getting out of the bath," I answered, coming out into the living room, pulling the ends of the belt on the bathrobe tight, feeling to make sure the neckline was overlapping around my metal collar as well. Then I casually went to the fridge and pulled out some wine. "Your mom has everything she needs?"

Since Ian slept with me every night at my place, it was easy enough to set his mom and her friends up at his place next door.

"They said they're good. The place is stocked with food, and they were all happy with the television and blankets. They also know we're next door if they need anything." He finally stood up, much to Kraken's dismay, and noted what I was doing. He cocked a brow, figuring out I was bent on getting him naked and inside me, and gave me just a hint of his sexy AF grin. "Wine?"

"I was thinking a snack before bed would be nice. Some wine. I also bought some strawberries at the farmer's market. The ends are already trimmed." And the tree lights were on casting a warm ambiance throughout the room. Some of them had a twinkling golden glow. It was perfect.

"Are you trying to seduce me, Blast?" His grin became a heated look, and he reached to snag a strawberry from across the bar. "You know I'm a sure thing, right?"

"I need to take care of my Hulk," I winked up at him and started pouring two glasses of white, but when I looked up at him, his expression had turned serious. The intensity was there, piercing with determination. There was something he needed to say.

"What is it?"

"We need to do some construction, make these two apartments into one." The determined look turned the statement into a demand. It wasn't a request. He was determined. We were maybe thinking on the same page here. My heart fluttered wildly as he added, "One door to come in for both of us. One key. Not two."

"Not just neighbors?" I asked, my eyes feeling shiny behind my glasses. We practically lived together anyway. Since our first night together, we hadn't spent a night apart, though most of his clothes were still at his place.

"I want more than that." He came around the counter and I turned to face him before he trapped me against it with his body. The strawberry I'd just washed was still between his fingers. He held it up to my lips for me to bite. A burst of sweetness lit my tongue, and I moaned. I licked my lips, and his gaze tracked that, a deep yearning in his eyes.

"What more do you want?" I asked, taking the strawberry from him and turning it around to give him the next bite.

"I want everything." His lips closed around the rest of the remaining fruit, inadvertently kissing my fingertips with his sexy lips before taking it into his mouth and chewing. He reached for another strawberry, holding it out for me to bite.

"Everything? Moving in together?" I asked, taking a bite.

"More."

I took the strawberry and held it up to his lips, my heart beating hard as I contemplated the next question. "G-getting m-married?" I still stumbled nervously on the word, a rush of nerves heating my face.

"More. Much more." This time when he leaned in for the bite, he let his tongue swirl around my fingertips before pulling it into his mouth. The pulse between my legs was growing stronger, a mixture of need and emotion that felt thick in my throat at the same time that they were carrying me to the very height of the stratosphere.

I blinked against the burn in my eyes. This time, instead of picking up a strawberry, he held up the wine glass to my lips. I sipped, savoring the words that were about to cross my lips.

"Having babies?" Little aquamarine-eyed babies running around? Playing with them on the beach? Our own little superheroes? I could see it in my mind. My breath hitched on a ball of emotion.

He sipped from the glass, his gaze fierce now, not leaving mine. "Yes. That. And more. So much more, Blast. Everything. Hopes, joys, pains, losses, babies, grandbabies. Everything. Forever."

The mental image of that was the most beautiful thing I could have pictured. The two of us. Always. Working together. Taking care of each other and anyone else that came along. I could see it already. It was not just right. It was perfect. The emotions rushed through me, eager to get out of my mouth and join the world we lived in.

"I love you, Ian. My Hulk," I choked up, words having to fight through the constriction in my throat. I was finally doing this.

His eyes burned into mine, making each word that much more important. "You'd better mean it because I've been in love with you since you put a curse on me." He set the wine glass down and cupped my face with both hands, his eyes drilling into mine. "I don't ever want you to lift that curse. Every day I revel in the feelings of being owned by you. I'm yours. Devoted to you. Utterly and completely. Your curse is my blessing."

"I do mean it," I whisper-chuckled as a tear dripped down my cheek. I hooked my hands over his biceps, swearing, "I'll never remove the curse. And it was my greatest wish and worst fear all at once. After spending so much time alone for my whole life, my greatest wish was to be with someone who wanted to design a beautiful life with me, but I was always afraid to actually let someone in because they couldn't see past the fact that I don't fit a mold. I'd figured I was too different and didn't have the magic ingredients to actually be able to love someone, but now I know I wasn't broken. I just hadn't met you."

The beautiful layers of color in this one moment were enough to keep me suspended as though this time were separate from reality. His thumb swiped the tear away. I was unable to look away from eyes I wanted to look into my entire life.

"You are my first step in chasing my own dreams, Blessing. We're going to have the best time. Best adventure together. I swear it. And you know what I'm like when I make a commitment. I'm never letting you go. Ever." He bent to caress my lips with his own, sealing the deal, his promise sinking into that ocean depth of my soul. Meeting me there. His arms snaked around my back, holding me close before he pulled away, giving me a quizzical look.

"What?" I asked.

"What are you wearing?"

He must have felt the chain hanging down my back when he hugged me. I gave him a sassy grin and moved around him with drama. Great sweeping steps and a come-hither smile that I flashed over my shoulder.

His eyes narrowed as he watched like a hawk, knowing I was up to something. He followed me, stood back as I faced him, ready to unveil myself. There was already a blanket set up on the thick rug in front of the tree. With that in mind, my fingers languidly unraveled the knot I'd created. Slowly, I let the robe fall to the floor.

It was worth it.

His jaw dropped.

He sucked in air as his eyes roamed my body hungrily.

His hand rubbed the front of his jeans, absently, adjusting the sudden tent that was growing against the more restrictive denim.

"Holy fuck, Blessing," he whispered, coming toward me. "You are so fucking hot. Do you know how often I have fantasized about this? Me and everything other straight man in the world."

I held up the end of the chain. The leash.

"Blast," he groaned, taking the end of the metal links attached to my neck and wrapping the slack around his fist. "You're going to make me come just from looking at you."

"We have all night." I looked up at him from beneath my lashes. "I'm your plaything."

"Blessing," he murmured reverently, pulling me closer using the chain in his one hand while caressing all of my exposed flesh with his other.

Then his fingers found the bikini top where the swells of my pale breasts were pushed up enticingly. He scooped my breast out and bent to lick the swollen nipple that popped free, rubbed it with his thumb to spread the shine he'd left with his mouth so that I was keening a soft moan.

I loved the newly familiar feeling of swollen heat in my nether regions. It felt like they were pulsing with molten fire. My arousal overwhelmed my senses anytime my Hulk gave me a heated look, much less touched me.

"You're a goddamn feast, Blast," he said darkly, moving from my peekaboo nipple up to my neck to kiss and suck at my skin before he was at my lips, a deep kiss filled with heat and need that had me threading my fingers into his hair to hold him in place. By the time his hands slid down my back and found my ass, kneading it while grinding his thick, massive length against my stomach, I was ready to throw him down and rip off his pants. As it stood, I was shoving his shirt up out of the way to get at his skin.

"Knees, Blast. I need your mouth," he commanded, yanking his shirt the rest of the way off.

I kneeled, willingly, getting off on the whole manhandling, making demands thing. On the way down, I sucked and kissed at the hard muscles of his abdomen, and the lines of his special V-shaped muscles that disappeared under the waistband of his jeans. Even took a few nipping bites that made his muscles clench tighter as he moaned his pleasure and anticipation.

Fuck, he was hot. It got me so fucking wet to see that look on his face and hear the sounds I inspired from him. This big man was about to lose control because of *me*.

"I need to take care of your monster, Hulk. He's become overgrown."

"He's insisting." Ian tilted his head to watch me, gave a partial grin, but his need was winning out in the clench of his jaw.

Reaching up, I unzipped him from his pants, and the monster was pulled free. Silky skin stretched taught over swollen steel heat. With reverence, I placed kisses on the head, licking at the precum as though it were icing on a cupcake. He was a little musky and salty. All him. I loved the taste of him and took him into my mouth.

"Fuck," he hissed, and his hips bucked. "Your mouth feels so good."

I bobbed on his cock, looking up at him holding that chain in his hand, and my pussy got hit with a sudden bolt of heat. My own fingers went between my legs to play as I sucked him off. He wasn't the only one who was owned. Watching him own me made me want to come hard. The need was twisting tighter and tighter, the waves of heat and arousal driving me higher.

"That's it, Blast, keep touching yourself. Make your pussy nice and wet for me." He was panting, sounding strained, watching me rub my clit with a look of tortured pleasure.

Licking a path down his shaft, I sucked on one of his balls, and there was a long, whispered "fuck" under his breath, his legs tensing, his hips thrusting, as he fucked my mouth. He was pulling on the chain rhythmically, groaning with each thrust until he used it to pull me off.

"Lay back," he growled suddenly, then proceeded to grab me by my waist and physically lay me back where he wanted me. His big, rough hands grabbed my thighs and spread them wide, as he kneeled between them. Then he pulled the curtain of burgundy costume material out of the way and saw that I was bare. Just waiting for him.

Another heartfelt groan left his chest before his fingers were there, thumbing my slit, invading my core, spreading the abundant slick that was being generated from my pussy.

"Always soaked for me. Aren't you, baby."

"Iaaaan," I moaned, panting heavily, trying to

grind on his fingers.

"You're so fucking hot I think about your beautiful little pussy all day. So pretty and swollen. I'm going to fuck it hard. I'm just warning you. But first, I need to French kiss your pussy again."

Then his face was between my legs, and after taking in my scent, he turned ravenous. Sucking at my clit had me crying out and grinding against his face. His tongue and lips were skilled, teasing and playing and getting me to the brink before backing off, over and over again. I was mindless, begging. Somewhere in there, he'd managed to shuck his jeans.

"I need you inside me. Please. Hulk. Please."

"I'll take care of you, baby."

And in seconds, he was kneeling between my legs, yanking them wide over his thighs before shoving a pillow under my ass for best angle. He lined up his cock with my pussy and slid balls deep instantly.

It was pure sensation. Filling me. Setting off nerve-endings that had my inner folds tightening around him.

"Oh, Blast," he groaned, his eyes closing with the ferocity of the pleasure. "Your pretty little pussy is gold. So hot. Tight." He moved his hips, thrusting his large length inside me. "Fuck, she squeezes down on me. She's my sweet little pussy. All mine." And he began to lengthen his strokes, grinding at the end of each one.

"Ian," I cried with each thrust. "It feels so good...!"

"Always, baby," he growled, reaching up to squeeze my tits and nipples with one hand, then sliding it down my abdomen so his thumb could strum my clit. He picked up the pace, and I got louder and louder until I was afraid Edie and her friends would hear us next door. I bit my lip to fight the cries that wanted to erupt.

"This pussy is mine, Blessing. I love this pussy. It's so pretty and perfect and wet as fuck." He was pounding into me now, the sweat building on his skin as I met him stroke for stroke. "I'm going to fuck her so good, so often, she'll only ever want to get wet for me."

His raspy words, the desperate look in his eyes, and the pressure his thumb was putting on my clit sent me tumbling over.

"I'm coming, I'm coming," I cried out in a fierce whisper, and then, it hit hard. My back arched, my legs shook, and I practically sobbed with the pleasure of it. Ian joined me there after thrusting half dozen more times, hard and fast, grunting with each motion of his hips until he, too, joined me in the aftermath, snarling his release and spurting hot cum deep inside me.

He collapsed on me after that. Still hard inside me. Both of us wrung out. He still placed gentle kisses along my temple.

Recovery took some time.

He rolled off me. Pulled the blanket over us. Anchored me half over him, and we gazed up at the Christmas tree lights, mindlessly floating on the feel-good chemicals we'd just saturated ourselves in. He stirred enough to run his fingers down over my ass, hold me in place, our legs intertwined.

"I was serious about what I said."

"Which parts?"

"All of it." He had his hand resting on my bare belly. "I want to see your belly grow with my spawn. I'm going to put a baby in you when the time is right."

"How many kids do you want?"

"At least five. We need creatures that we can train to take over the evil empire we'll eventually build."

"How about we start with a couple, and see where that leads?"

"I can live with that."

I leaned up on my elbow to look him in the eye.

"In no way is this me saying yes to marriage."

He scowled. "What do you mean?"

"I mean, you still owe me a proposal."

The scowl morphed back into a relaxed smile.

"Oh, you'll get your proposal, my Bomb Blast. Count on it."

Epilogue
Bethany

"You always look so fabulous!"

Blessing air-kissed my cheek with that pronouncement. The scent of fruity alcohol was on her breath, a carefree grin on her face. My new friend had downed a few. But why the hell not? It was New Years' Eve, this was a private party, and she wasn't driving anywhere.

It was just strange to be the one doing the serving on a party night. I was used to being served. Shit. I was used to being the life of the party.

What a difference a day made.

"Thank you, Bless," I grinned when she slung an arm over my shoulders. Damn, she was a goofy drunk. "Just a little something I made for myself."

We were all at Zeke's on the Boardwalk celebrating not only the New Year, but the completion of Blessing's game. It was steampunk themed, which had inspired me to make my own outfit for tonight, even if I was working. It didn't all have to be dreary.

"You make your own clothes? You look so fucking amazing," she enthused, running a careless hand over the material on my chest, nearly copping an unexpected feel, but I was cool with it. It wasn't like anyone else was touching me these days. No action in this neck of the woods. But she wasn't finished. She added, "Like, so fucking amazing. Fits you so perfectly."

Yup. Drunk. Goofy grin.

Still, I looked down at the tailoring I'd done to create the deep, emerald-green vest that peeked out of a matching waist-length, fitted top-coat. It outlined the plunging V-neck of my fitted white button-up that showcased one of the best things about me: My abundant tits.

"It's a hobby of mine." I appreciated the compliment, in all honesty.

"You are so fucking talented," she said with a little more groping as she took a closer look at the workmanship. "You have to make me one of these. Seriously. It would drive Ian nuts, and that would end up making me a very happy girl. You catch my drift?"

"More than," I smirked, glancing over at her man. He was talking with Mason, but his eyes were burning a hole in her back, keeping track of what she was doing. He had the whole protective vibe going.

In truth, sewing was no big deal to me. I'd been making my own clothes since about middle school where I'd not only learned to sew in one of the last Home Ec. classes in the state, but I'd also learned that my very wealthy stepfather was leaving my mother to move on to the secretary that had taken her place. Thirteen was not a good age for me in some ways, but amazing in others. With money tighter, I'd learned how to follow the sewing patterns from houses of haute couture that I found online and made my own damn clothes.

That's why I always looked good.

I shook off the memory. It brought me down, and I had a rule about myself. Anything that could bring me down, I shook off. Dusted off what I didn't want to have stick. No one would ever think I suffered from static cling because my natural default was to look for something new. Bad things were deleted, and then I moved on. Easy.

"You have got to do our costumes for Comic-Con! Seriously! I have drawings. We'll make the biggest fucking splash ever! They'll be remembering us for years! I'm going to call you to arrange a meeting because, damn girl, you are amazing. I have your number," Blessing was nodding eagerly.

"For sure," I said automatically, knowing that what people said when they were drunk was rarely remembered.

"Hey Princess," Magnus called rudely from behind the bar.

I fought the urge to grit my teeth, and instead, air-kissed Blessing's cheek in return. "You deserve this, girlfriend. All of it."

"All of it," she agreed merrily, taking out her phone. "So much. Fuck me, girlfriend. I did something cool."

"I'm going to leave the fucking to Ian, but I catch your drift."

"He does fuck me good," she giggled, not realizing her words were louder than she realized. "He fucks me really, really, good."

"Blast," Ian suddenly appeared behind her. "You spilling our secrets?"

"No way! Never," she shook her head and winked at me. "Make sure you have my number!"

"Princess!" Magnus barked again.

"Have fun and drink some water," I offered before adding darkly, "I have some balls to break."

"Keep it legal!"

"Where's the fun in that?" I smirked, and for a moment was feeling a lightness that I wondered if I'd ever felt before. More and more, lately, I could smile and be happy. Was it due to having friends? Real friends who seemed to give a shit about me.

Did that make the difference? Blessing and Layla were actual friends. Not chicks who were looking for a weakness to exploit. No, they were honest friends who went out of their way to help me when I didn't deserve an ounce of their consideration after all the shit I pulled, acting like such a bitch, which I'd also totally apologized for.

Yet another first.

"Bethany," he growled when I approached. For some reason, his tone of voice made me shiver, but that was wrong. He was an ass. I'd never do him. So I ignored the feeling."

"What is it, peon?"

He narrowed his forest green eyes at me. "These orders aren't going to serve themselves. Worry about your fan club later."

And that's when I'd had it. I stalked around the bar, pushing up into his ear to hiss, "What is your problem with me? All of the customers are happy, and I'm getting the orders out in a reasonable time."

He pulled back, a hard look in his eyes. "I don't have a problem with you."

"Oh yes, you do." I looked him up and down, hating that he was my type. Muscled. Tatted. Military grade haircut and a beard. Gruff asshole. It was hard not to feel attracted. As a result, I snarled, "Don't be such a goddamn pussy. Talk already. What's your problem with me?"

"Fine. You want to know?" He tossed the bar

towel down on his workspace and squared off with me. "My problem with you is that you only ever think about you. When it doesn't go your way, you pull the lynch pin on the grenade, even if it ends up blowing you up, too, because you are entirely self-centered."

"Fucking asshole." I snarled, the shame of his words striking exactly the right chord and making my face flush. "You want to do all this alone?" I started backing off with a triumphant smile.

"Exactly. You make my point," he looked grim. "Fucking middle school girl behavior. See you, Bethany. Don't let the door hit your ass when you leave."

He wasn't going to chase me out. Try to get me to stay. He was going to work his ass off for the rest of the night because I would leave him understaffed for the occasion. It suddenly occurred to me that this was a pivotal moment. This was a moment where I could cause him to permanently view me in a way that we would never come back from.

For some reason, that made me pause. Think this through.

I was about to walk out. Leave him to fuck this all up with drinks piling up and not enough help, but then came the realization that I wouldn't just be affecting him. I would be fucking up Blessing's celebration. There was no way I wanted to screw over Blessing.

As much as I hated Magnus in this moment, I knew he was right. I'd been about to storm off in high fashion because he'd insulted me. And I wasn't missing the irony that he'd only done it because I badgered him into admitting he had a problem with me. And it wasn't even an insult. It was truth. Something few people in my life had offered me.

Fuck.

Was I going to keep sinking to meet his, and everyone's, lowered expectations of me, or was I going to start requiring more of myself? Grow the fuck up, finally. Which was hard because I did have knee jerk reaction. I knew this. I was prone to tantrums. Maybe I needed to take the advice I gave Blessing. Pull up my own big girl panties.

But it didn't have to remain this way.

It was time to recognize my house of cards. The life I'd built for myself had been entirely artificial and had left me completely vulnerable. I was tired of needing someone else in order to live. I didn't want to *need* anymore. Always living "in need" took away my ability to find someone I *wanted*. Or not. Who said I needed to be with anyone? Wasn't that a crazy idea? Maybe not so crazy.

Maybe I could find the life I wanted.

It was time to change the rules in my life. Do some things different.

I grabbed the tray of orders and started

delivering them around the party, hating that I really liked the nod of respect Magnus offered when I made that choice.

***

Thanks so much for reading FIERY BLESSING! I hope you loved reading Blessing and Ian's story as much as I loved writing it. They were fun, quirky, sexy characters who practically wrote this story themselves.

***

Bethany and Magnus are next! Preorder DIAMONDS ON THE WATER to follow Bethany and Magnus who fight fiercely against their inconvenient, off the charts, explosive chemistry in this enemies to lovers story. She thinks he's a rude, grumpy tyrant, and he thinks she's a high maintenance, entitled princess. Neither of them is totally wrong nor totally right. However, for the first time, Bethany's getting paid for a secret passion she's always had: her clothing creations. Magnus reluctantly respects her determination and drive. Will he give in to his deepest, darkest need to claim her, or will he possibly lose the best thing that ever happened to him? Find DIAMONDS ON THE WATER on AMAZON to preorder.

***

If you missed Layla and Mason's story, read it now!
Find ONE BREATH TO THE NEXT on AMAZON
to see where it all started:

She wanted Mason Garrett, so she made him an offer he couldn't refuse...

Mason is ex-military with PTSD and torturous secrets that are forever locked in his mind. He isolates himself from attachments at the same time that his dark, brooding gaze tracks Layla, the girl he's silently obsessed with. Then one day, she comes to him with a proposal.

Layla is fiercely single, a survivor of her own past, but when a single look from Mason makes her body burn with newfound desire, she finds the courage to approach him. Her offer? Sex with no strings, no hearts, no flowers. Definitely no commitment.

It seems the perfect arrangement, unless their hearts decide they are perfect for each other.

This book is hot, hot, hot with steamy scenes! Lots of good feels. No cheating and guaranteed HEA. Heroine has a few short moments where she remembers past abuse, so if you find this to be a sensitive topic, it may not be the book for you.

***

If you enjoyed reading this series, you would love Kat and Beck's story in <u>WINTER HEAT</u>, available now from AMAZON!

A snowy cabin in the woods, a stubborn woman hellbent on hiding from the truth, and a brooding, determined male... Now throw in some convenient handcuffs.

Cat is handcuffed to me until she faces the truth: She's always been mine.

Our group of friends, our chosen family, is meeting for the holidays at a cabin in the mountains. This is where it's going down. The ridiculous lies she's been telling herself will be faced head-on, and she'll be out of excuses. I won't allow her to hide anymore.

She might have run because the woman has trust issues, but I plan to catch her and keep her forever.

Find <u>WINTER HEAT</u> on AMAZON to start reading!

****I PROMISE, there is NO CHEATING, but there is deep love, and lots of steamy, sexy moments.

BOOKS BY DANUBE ADELE

KISS AND TELL

Winter Heat, *#1, Kat and Beck*
Truth or Dare, *#2 Simone and Topher*

HERMOSA BEACH MEMOIRS

One Breath to the Next, *#1, Layla and Mason*
Fiery Blessing, *#2, Blessing and Ian*
Diamonds on the Water, *#3, Bethany and Magnus*

ABOUT THE AUTHOR

Danube Adele believes that a good nap can solve most problems, diving into new adventure kickstarts creativity, and quiet walks along the beach soothe the soul. Add a mango margarita paired with chips and salsa to the mix, and you get a happy life. Author of the paranormal, sci-fi romance series Dreamwalkers, new contemporary series Hermosa Beach Memoirs, and steamy novella duet from the Kiss and Tell series, she can often be found either eagerly typing away at an HEA on her laptop, or lounging on the sofa with a hot, sexy romance novel in hand. She's lived in southern California her entire life, and much of that time with her greatest fans, her loving husband and two brilliant sons.

Sign up for Danube Adele's newsletter

Like Danube Adele on:

Facebook

Goodreads

Bookbub

Twitter

.

Made in the USA
Middletown, DE
28 December 2021